REDEMPTION (Nashville Nights, #3)

Holding on never felt so good.

Emory Cabell is leaving the lies behind her.

Finding out that you're the half-sister to America's country music queen is game changer. Determined to meet the sibling she never knew and compelled to pursue the music career she's always wanted, Emory leaves her small town and heads to Nashville. Thrown by the bustle of Music City and the cutthroat dealing of the business, she finds unexpected shelter in a musical partnership with country music's notorious bad boy.

Zane has his eyes set on the prize.

Known as a man who never stays the night, Zane is reliable only when it comes to his music. Years of paying his dues has gained him the coveted lead guitarist spot on the hottest music tour of the year. Hoping this gig will lead to his own recording contract, he agrees to write a few songs with Emory but he's blown away by the sexual chemistry sizzling between them and leveled by his feelings for this quiet woman with the beautiful soul.

Can love be more than just a line in a song?

Darkness and light... they should not work. But one night in her bed proves they're hotter than the number one single they wrote together. Things get complicated when the spotlight sheds light on all of Zane's past sins and Emory struggles with trusting him with her heart. When the sought after recording contract stipulates they remain a duet, it threatens everything Zane has worked towards and challenges everything he thought he knew about himself. With his life at a crossroads, will he choose the music or the future with a woman whose love might just be his redemption?

REDEMPTION

BY

ROBIN COVINGTON

Holding On Never Felt So Good

Burning Up the Sheets, LLC
23139 Laurel Way
Hollywood, MD 20636

Visit my website at www.robincovingtonromance.com.
Cover design by Sweet & Spicy Designs.

Ebook ISBN: 978-0-9905432-4-4
Print ISBN: 978-0-9905432-6-8

Manufactured in the United States of America
First Edition June 2015

Chapter One

Zane

I should have stayed at my place last night. I'm dangerously close to being late.

I slither out of bed, moving arms and legs gently out of my way, careful not to wake my bedmates. Angie mumbles in her sleep and rolls over, her movement jostling her husband and I freeze, hoping they will not wake up. I'm not worried about awkward moments and the walk of shame because I have nothing to be embarrassed about. I just don't have time to spend on any kind of goodbye.

Angela and Bobby Graves are a happily married couple who occasionally invite a third to their bed and lately that extra body has been me. As a rule, while I don't have many scruples about sleeping around, I draw the line at banging married women whose husbands are not part of the invitation. What arrangement they have between them is none of my business but I'm not interested in making some guy look like an asshole.

I'm also not interested in letting everyone in Nashville know where I sleep and how many people are in the bed at the time. The country music business puts up with my tattoos, my love of using the word "fuck" in as many ways as possible, and the sleeping around one woman at a time. A threesome would make their heads explode and I don't need any of the record label executive's brains spattering their office wall before they sign me to a solo record deal.

I worked my ass off for the last five years, hitting the pavement the second I got off the bus in Nashville to start college on a scholarship at Nashville University. I auditioned at record labels before I made sure I had the classes I needed and spent more time writing songs than doing my homework. My name as a guy who can write a Top Ten song is solid and I used it to build a name as a performer and to finally land the gig as Kit Landry's lead guitarist and opening act on her sold-out summer tour.

The tour I'm going to miss if I don't get my ass out of here and on the bus waiting for me in downtown Nashville.

I lean over to scoop my boxer briefs and jeans off the floor, balancing myself on one foot as I struggle to get dressed silently.

"Nice ass," Angie mumbles from where she lies nestled in the one thousand thread count sheets. She doesn't make a move to get up and I don't move towards her. This isn't about goodbye kisses or promises to call. We're friends but there are definite boundaries and we never cross them. I have no desire to.

"Well you can kiss it goodbye until September," I chuckle as I pull my jeans up and button the fly. She sticks her tongue out at me and I roll my eyes as tug my t-shirt over my head. "You guys are coming to one of the Nashville shows, right?"

"Bobby's company has a block of seats. We'll be there."

I nod and pull my shoulder-length hair back with an elastic I had in my pocket. Bobby's an executive at a big IT firm and like most successful Music City corporations they buy blocks of seats to wine and dine clients.

"I'll see you at the show," I back out of the room and give her a wave, not offering VIP passes or making any promises. With her job as a top pediatric surgeon at the largest area hospital and Bobby's high-profile career, they don't like to leave too many paper trails between us. That's fine with me.

I jog out to my car parked in the third garage slot of their gated-community mansion and back out once the door goes up. Nobody is up this early in the morning so I don't worry about raising too many eyebrows as I exceed the speed limit and make my way through the sleepy Nashville streets to the house I share with my best friend, Mateo Butler.

I used the terms "share" loosely now because he spends any time he's not in medical school or working at the free clinic with his girlfriend, Carlisle Queen. I see her exclusive building on the skyline as I drive by and offer a silent salute to the two of them. True love if I ever saw it. Just because I'm not looking for it doesn't mean I don't know it.

And it sure as fuck doesn't mean that I can't write a song about it. Thank God.

I pull into the cracked concrete driveway next to our rental house on the edge of the Nashville University campus, kill the engine and bolt into the house. I check the time. I've got enough time to take a shower and grab the duffle I packed last night.

With wet hair, a travel mug of coffee and a KIND bar in hand, I throw my bag into the trunk of the cab and pile into the back with my guitar and direct the cabbie to head to the parking lot near the rehearsal spaces of Kit's record label. When I pull into the lot, the buses are lined up and people are wandering around the lot like zombies looking for brains.

My blood pressure spikes as my feet hit the pavement and the familiar jolt of excitement builds up in my chest until I fully expect it to shoot out my fingertips. I love writing and performing, going on the road for several months and the prospect of playing in huge, sold-out arenas is giving me a boner that's making jeans tight. And on this tour in addition to the lead guitarist spot I get to be an opening act in many of the cities.

I can almost feel the pen in my hand as I sign the recording contract.

"Mac, are you ready my man?" I roll up beside the drummer, Mac Giles, and we fist bump both grinning ear-to-ear. Mac is a road junkie like me, loves the crowds and playing to a full house. We'll be riding together on the band bus along with the bassist, Aaron Rice, and the keyboardist, Mike Leonard. With these four guys I predict lots of X-box tournaments and jam sessions and I can't fucking wait.

"Zane, this shit is going to be awesome." He nudges me with one of his beefy arms and grins. "Sold out tour mother fucker."

I grin back. "Sold out tour mother fucker."

"Did you even roll out of your own bed this morning?" He eyeballs me as we make our way over to our bus. "What did you do? Give her a nine-inch wake-up call and make it home in time just to shower and grab coffee?"

"Something like that," I answer, refusing to kiss and tell my playmate's secrets. "I packed last night so it was all good."

"If you get as much tail as you did last summer, your dick is going to fall off," he warns, his smile evil as he continues. "And I'll be there to soothe all the sad "pick collectors.""

"That was just that group of rabid fan club girls in Utah and I know better than to leave my stash lying around where they can get their hands on it." I lost an entire case of custom-made copper guitar picks when my hookup in Salt Lake City stole them and then sold them on E-bay. I will never make that mistake again. "Those picks aren't fucking cheap."

"Those Utah girls were freaky," Mac smiles as he shakes his head. We played three nights there and it was everything you hear about concert tours.

"Well, apparently what they say about the quiet ones is true," I say and stop when I bump into his large frame. "What the fuck, Mac?"

I turn my head to see what is causing his slack-jawed staring and when I do I understand completely. Emory Cabell. Backup singer. Exquisite guitarist. Honey blonde with legs that go on for miles and breasts that would fit perfectly in my palms.

And Kit Landry's new-found baby sister.

We both ogle as she bends over and tries to lift a heavy suitcase. Emory is wearing cutoff jean shorts, a little red t-shirt and flip-flops. Her legs are endless and the cutoffs are just short enough to give a hint of the sweet little curve of her ass.

"Oh my God," Mac says, his voice strained with the same tension I feel in my body.

"Fuckin-A." I shift slightly to redistribute the half-hard boner in my jeans and barely bite back the laugh that is bubbling in my chest. God was not kind when he put Emory Cabell on my path. She's a walking wet dream pulled right out my fantasy archive and she's so off-limits that she might as well live on Alcatraz but my dick is ignoring the memo.

We watch for a few moments longer as she struggles with the multiple pieces of luggage she's trying to get on the bus she will share with Kit and the other back-up singer, Sandra. I shove my own duffle at Mac, ignoring his grunt of pain as it plows into his abdomen.

"I should go help her," I say.

"No, you shouldn't."

"She needs my help. It's the right thing to do."

"Just remember that helping her does not require anyone to remove their clothes."

"And *that* is a fucking shame," I answer. I walk towards her, approaching from the side. The way she's heaving around the smaller bag it's become a dangerous weapon, so I reach out and grab it when I get within range. She pops her head up, eyes wide with surprise. We stare at each other for a few seconds longer than necessary and the all-to-familiar heat that simmers between us makes the emerald in her gaze catch fire. Yeah, there's something between me and this girl. "Let me help you with that before you put someone's eye out."

Emory hesitates for a second and then nods in relief and shoves the bag into my hand.

"I think I over packed," she grunts as she grasps the handle on her rolling case and positions it to move towards the door. I lean over and pick up a backpack and her guitar case but her hand on my arm stops me. She bypasses the backpack but takes the instrument from me. "I'll take this."

"I get it. I don't like anyone messing with my guitar either."

She smiles at me and I'm struck again with just how

sweet she is. A nice girl. Not innocent; she's held her own with everyone during the rehearsal time, matching dirty joke for dirty joke and cussing like a sailor when it was required. No, she's fresh and open and completely unvarnished by this business. We all start out the same way and I regret that one day she'll be a cold bastard like me when it comes to non-musical side of this gig. Luckily, she has her sister to look out for her.

"I set my alarm super early and I still found myself scrambling to get here on time," she huffs out as she rolls the larger case towards the door.

I squeeze past her and grab the handle, hefting it up the steps into the bus and setting it just inside the opening. I place the backpack on the floor next to it before turning back to her. She's moved in behind me and now she's close enough for me to see the gold flecks in her eyes and smell whatever citrus scent she wears. She's even prettier up close and my mouth goes a little bit dry.

"I did the same thing," I confess. "This is my second time on this kind of tour and you'd think that I'd know better."

"If you started the morning out in your own bed you might not have been so strapped for time," Kit says, appearing in the doorway, smiling like the annoying sister who knows she just cock blocked you with her hot friend. I love her, I really do, but I want to throttle her right now.

Emory laugh and slaps her hand against her mouth. "Kit!"

"Now, that was just mean," I say, smiling and leaning up to kiss Kit on her cheek as Emory continues to laugh at us.

"But, you aren't denying it," Kit shoves me playfully and I stumble back, placing my hand over my heart in an action that mimics someone suffering from a shot to the gut.

"Kit, that was pretty harsh," Emory chastises her sister and leans over to pat me on the head with a smile. Her touch is supposed to be soothing but it is exactly the opposite. I would love to have her hands on me without so many other people around.

"Zane Wyatt you're a horny dog of the first order and you know it." Kit looks at her sister after winking at me. "Don't be fooled just because he's my favorite stray."

"Hey, I'm housebroken and I only bite on special occasions," I protest lightly.

I'm not offended by her words. Kit is engaged to one of my closest friends who is also the cousin of my best friend, so we've spent a lot of time together the last couple of years. If it wasn't for her and the Butlers, I wouldn't have any family where I can be myself. It's the main reason why I haven't really tried anything with Emory. That shit could get complicated really fast.

"It's a good thing I've got all my shots then," Emory interrupts my thoughts, her soft voice low and teasing with more than a hint of the suggestive. She gives me a lingering look before easing past Kit to enter the tour bus. I stare after her and it takes a few moments before I realize that Kit is still standing in the same place, her expression equal parts concerned and resigned.

"It won't do any good to remind you that she's my sister, would it?"

I swallow hard, deciding to go with honesty. "Probably not."

She nods. "I didn't think so."

I wait for the rest of the lecture to follow and I when I realize that it isn't coming I have to ask. "What? You aren't going to forbid me to hang out with your sister. Threaten to have Max break my legs if I touch her?"

"If I thought it would do any good, I would." She sighs and descends the steps to speak directly to me, her hand resting lightly on my arm. "I would have to be blind and stupid to miss the sparks between the two of you. I have no right to tell you guys what to do but I'm asking you to treat her right. Don't lead her on. Be straight with her."

"I am always honest with the women I'm with."

"I know and that's why I'm not putting a hit out on you

right now. She's not some dumb kid from the sticks, she's smart and cautious and way more mature than I was when I came here but she's looking for something and that makes her vulnerable."

Alarm bells go off in my head. Depending on what she's looking for, I have no idea if I can deliver.

"What is she looking for, Kit?"

"I'm not even sure she knows what it is yet." Kit squeezes my arm before backing off and getting on the bus. "Just be careful Zane. You're both my family."

And right then I decide that if I'm smart, I'll never lay a finger on Emory Cabell.

Chapter Two

Emory

"I love Zane like a brother."

I stop unpacking my things and placing them in the storage compartment under my bed on the bus to look at my new half-sister. Kit is leaning against the outer wall of the bunk, her fingers twisting around each other. That outward demonstration of agitation matches the concern in her eyes and I sigh as I drop my clothes and straighten. I end up looking down on her since I'm a good five inches taller than her petite size but it doesn't faze her. She's in a full-on big sister mode and that makes her ten feet tall.

"Why do I know there's an unspoken 'but' at the end of that sentence?" I say.

"Because there is," she says, reaching out to lay a hand on my arm. "He's hands down one of the best songwriters in this town and I'd pit his guitar skills up against John Mayer or Keith Urban any day. He's funny and helpful and he is a dear friend but he sleeps with everything that moves."

"That's not news, Kit. It was one of the first pieces of information everyone offered up when rehearsals started. The people in your band are bigger gossips than a bunch of high school girls."

"Tell me something I don't know." Kit slides onto the bunk and pats the mattress to invite me to sit next to her.

I hesitate, still not sure about where we are going with this relationship. Kit has been amazing ever since I contacted her manager, Paul Brandt, with the news that we shared a daddy six months ago. The realization that *her daddy* had a second, secret family and was *my daddy* when he was supposedly on "long trucking runs" served as the initial glue that bound us together. Whether we actually become a family of our own for the long-term is still up for anybody's guess but so far it's gone way better than it probably should. I grew up an only child and the prospect of having a sister is more appealing than I'd like to admit.

This tour is a way to help us grow closer and to allow me to see if the music business is what I really want. Up until six months ago I'd lived my entire life in Dutton, Tennessee, a small, podunk place outside of Memphis. My only visits to Nashville were with school trips and for special occasions. My dreams of making a life out of my music were secrets I only told myself until the realization that nothing in my past was true compelled me to find my own future.

Now I'm living in Kit's old loft in downtown and singing back-up on her sold out tour. The last time this much had changed so fast for a girl, Alice drank the wrong the bottle and ended up down a rabbit hole. There are days when I think the Mad Hatter is just around the corner.

"So, are you pulling the "big sister" card and telling me to stay away from him?" I ask as I slide into the bunk beside her. Our backs are against the wall and our feet are dangling off the edge. I wonder if this what we would have done if we'd grown up together.

"Oh, hell no," she laughs and looks at me. "I know better than to challenge your stubborn streak. You get that from daddy and I will not awaken that sleeping beast. I'm a firm believer that you need to make your own decisions, good or bad."

I wait. I know there's a "but". It's practically hanging over her head like a neon sign.

"I don't want to see you get hurt, Em. I know firsthand how a body blow like this can cloud your judgment and you already had one this year."

She isn't exaggerating. You can Google "Kit Landry" and get a front row seat for all the mistakes she made the year after a devastating break-up.

"It all ended up great for you in the end," I point out. "Your career is stellar and you have that big ass rock on your finger and a hot guy who adores you."

She smiles the goofy grin that always shows up when you bring up her man, Max Butler. At the end of this tour they're getting married and I swear that if you look up "happily ever after" in the dictionary, it points to them. I know that kind of love is real. I believe it's possible but I can't shake the thought that you never really know anybody and to put all your happiness in one person might not be a smart idea. The best acting isn't only done in Hollywood.

My daddy fooled us right up to the day he died and now I don't know whether to trust anybody, including myself.

Kit appears to read my thoughts and reaches down to squeeze my hand. "It will all work out for you too, Em. You wouldn't have found me and come to Nashville if you didn't have the guts to get the life you want."

I lean my head back on the wall of the bus and close my eyes. "What life do I want?"

"That's not a question I can answer for you little sister."

"I know what I *don't* want."

"That's a start. Give me the list."

"Lies. Insecurity. Doubt. My old boring life." I hear Kit suck in a quick breath and I realize that I might have over-shared. Dr. Phil would be all over me right now. I decide to lighten it up. "A minivan. I don't want a minivan. Or white heels. Nobody should wear white heels."

"Wow. That's a wide range of stuff. Your issues are like a Super-Walmart."

"Daddy and trust issues. Clean up on Aisle Three," I joke.

The silence that settles between us is comfortable. Kit doesn't feel like she needs to fill the silence or fix my life. She's cool just being here. I like that...a lot. I didn't have lots of girlfriends growing up. Mom was too weird and I always felt like I had one foot out of the metaphorical door of that tiny little town. I didn't want to make attachments I'd have to give up.

"I know that I want the music. Thanks for the opportunity," I say.

"You didn't get here because you're my sister," she starts and then corrects herself with a laugh. "Okay, you got your ass in the door with zero experience because you're my sister but you wouldn't have gotten a back-up spot if you didn't have a voice that makes me want to kill you."

I nudge her with an elbow. "Whatever."

"You're also an amazing guitarist."

I motion in the air with my finger, giving her the "keep it coming" gesture. "Talk about my looks and my day will be complete."

She rolls her eyes. "You're gorgeous and you know it. I would kill for your legs."

"You have great legs." She really does. She's petite with dark curls with red streaks in it. There's a reason her cover of *Rolling Stone* is one of the most popular.

"I'm stumpy compared to you." She eyeballs me and shakes her head. "We look nothing alike. Did daddy contribute anything to our DNA at all?"

"The music. He gave us the music."

We stare at each other for several long seconds. The silent "thank God" remains unsaid but hovers between us.

"He did give us that." She leans over and kisses me on the cheek before moving to scoot out of the bunk. "Speaking of the music, I want you to work with Zane and see how you like songwriting. I think you two might have a good sound together."

"I thought I was supposed to avoid him?"

"Writing a song doesn't entail taking off any clothing."

"That's a shame." I mean it. I don't have a ton of experience with seeing men unclothed but I know enough to believe that seeing Zane Wyatt naked might just be the experience of a lifetime. He's hot and sexy and crazy talented. An irresistible combination. There's a reason that musicians

16

get laid a lot.

"It's the hands. Women love the hands," I speculate.

"It's his hair. Women love his hair," she adds.

"His hair is pretty spectacular. Shoulder-length, dark and always messy like he just rolled out of bed."

"I think I should be worried that you've given it so much thought," she says her smile now dampened with a little bit of concern. "He's a great guy but he isn't the commitment type, so if you get involved with him just understand the law of the land."

I have no idea if I'm looking for a relationship or not. I'm in a new life and playing it all by ear. What comes my way will be considered and if I want to leap, I will. I've spent a lifetime living in a box constructed of other people's expectations and now I'm determined to stay out of that box. I'm open to anything and I really only have one, real hot button.

"Is he honest?"

Kit considers me for a long moment. She knows where I'm coming from. My showing up in her life just added another layer of suck to the memories of her already sucktastic childhood. Neither of us relish the fact that our father lied to us our entire lives. So, there are a lot of things I can tolerate but lying isn't one of them.

"He is. He won't play games with you. Just remember, the only thing he really commits to is his career."

"Got it." I flop down on my bunk and watch her exit the bus.

Tired from a night of tossing and turning from excitement, I settle back against the covers, staring up at the ceiling and once again wondering just how the hell I ended up here. Six months ago I was living in Dutton and now I am here against the wishes of everyone in my life: mama, Eric, the entire town. Even the cashier at the Piggly Wiggly had an opinion about my decision to move to the big, bad city.

But I'm here.

Indulging in my passion for music. Traveling all over the

country. Figuring out what the hell I want to do with my life.

Contemplating the delicious possibility of getting naked with a very sexy guitarist.

Life just got very, very interesting.

Chapter Three

Zane

"So, Kit wants us to try writing a song together."

I look up from where I sit on the floor of the stage, checking the strings on my guitar to find Emory smiling down at me. She's holding her guitar in one hand and wearing this tiny little dress that slips off one of her pale shoulders. I can see the light sprinkling of freckles along her collarbone and I bite back the urge to connect the dots with my tongue. Fuck, but she makes me want.

"Yes, she does." I cock my head at her, trying to gauge her reaction to the suggestion. "I think it might be a very cool thing to try. How about you?"

"I'd love it," she says, the pretty blush on her cheeks giving away her excitement. It's one of the things I like most about Emory; her enthusiasm for new things. She's brave and takes chances even when you can tell it scares her shitless.

"Are you doing anything right now?" I ask, standing up to be able to look at her in the eyes instead of putting a permanent kink in my neck. "We could find a spot, talk, get to know each other a little bit better."

"Do we need to know each other better to write a song?"

"No, but it doesn't hurt." I look around the stage tossing around the possible areas where we could work without interruptions. I shiver a little under the onslaught of air conditioning they are pouring into this place in preparation for the thousands of bodies that will be cram in here tonight and I know where I want to go. "You want to go outside? There's an area to the side of the stadium with picnic tables and shade trees. We can enjoy the sun."

"I like that idea."

We cut through the backstage area, making sure to avoid the guys working out the last minute electrical and sound kinks. We exit the building through the artist entrance and I lead her over to the little picnic area tucked along the back of the arena complex. It's empty and quiet. Perfect.

"Okay. Good choice," she hums in approval as she climbs on top of one of the tables and kicks off her flip flops. She places her guitar beside her on the flat surface and leans back, her face lifted to the sun. I stare. It's not a casual glance. I take my time and ogle the slender length of her neck and indulge in the fantasy of tasting her there. She looks up suddenly and busts me. Cold.

"I was staring," I confess, letting her see that I'm really not sorry.

"I noticed," she says, cocking her head to the side with her eyebrows raised in a question. The hint of a smile on her lips tells me that she's not offended by my behavior and isn't going to beat me over the head with the instrument siting within her arm's length. "Is your staring part of the 'getting to know you' thing we're supposed to be doing?"

"Yep. It is." I hop up on the table next to her, my guitar placed on the bench at my feet. "Writing music together is not just about notes and lyrics. It's about the dynamic between two people, the way you interact."

"And our dynamic involves you checking me out?"

"And *you* checking me out," I say and smile when she huffs out a sound of protest. "Come on, we're attracted to each other. We might as well just put it out there."

She laughs and nods, looking down at her feet as they swing off the edge of the table. I wait to see what her next move will be, anxious for a clue about where her head is. Emory looks up at me, her green eyes bright with curiosity that I want to pursue so badly my teeth ache.

"And what do we do with this attraction? Give into it?"

"We can." I reach out to brush her hair back off her face

where the light breeze blocks my view of her expression. I need to see all of it. "Or we can do nothing. Either way, it will be powerful to channel it into a song."

"Do you sleep with everyone you write a song with?" Emory pauses for a moment and clarifies her question. "The women, I mean."

"First, there's no hard and fast rule. I sleep with people I'm attracted to when it feels right, no matter the gender." I pause to let that sink in and when I all get from her is an eyebrow raise and a smile, I continue with the rest of my theory. "Sometimes the attraction is just the music. All the emotion and heat all feeds into the song and then there's nothing left."

"And where do we fall into the spectrum?"

"Not sure yet but I know we've got enough going on that the music will probably be amazing."

She smiles and looks down, running her fingers over the strings of her guitar. "I like the honesty, Zane. Where I'm from there's a lot of talking around things."

"And you don't like that?"

"I hate it," she says and lifts her eyes to mine, her expression interested and open. "So, what is your grand plan, Zane? Lead guitarist and songwriter or world music domination?"

"Who told you?" I laugh and ease back to lean on my elbows across the table. "I want my own record deal and I'm so close to getting it I can almost smell the ink on the contract. My agent is talking to a couple of labels but they're waiting to see how my opening slot for this tour goes."

"Well, you've been amazing, getting great reviews. You'll get it."

"It all depends on the type of offer. I want a 360 deal with primary creative control. I've got the music; I just need their marketing money and reach to make me a global brand. These days there isn't much that a record label can do for you that you can't do for yourself if you work hard enough and use social media."

"Have you had an offer on the table before? Is that something a new artist could expect to get?" She pushes a blonde curl behind her ear and smiles in apology. "Sorry. I'm a total newbie and all of this fascinates me."

"No worries. Ask away. I had a deal last year from this smaller Indie label called Waterworld Media but they wanted more creative control than I wanted to give up. The owner, Maureen Richards, also wanted personal control over *me* but I didn't want to be the owner's toy of the moment even for a record deal."

"Is that how it usually works or is that just a thing I've seen on TV? Kit never told me about having to sleep with people to make it."

"Kit didn't and she was lucky to have Paul Brandt looking after her and protecting her when she was so young. Just remember that sex is a commodity that the majority of the people have no problem using." I pull a guitar pick out of my pocket and twist it between my fingers. "I'm also not talking about two people who both happen to be in this business who also want to hook-up. There's a difference between indulging in sex for pleasure and whoring around. Sex always complicate things but you don't want it to mess up your career."

"I hear ya. It's why I'm still a virgin."

I stare at her, not quite sure I heard what I heard.

"You're a what?"

She turns her head to look at me, squinting at the sun in her eyes. "A virgin. Untouched. Still holding my V-card."

"Umm. Now I feel like dirty old man." I take a good look at her and ask the question I'm not sure I want to know the answer to. It just never occurred to me to ask. "Wait. How old are you, Emory?"

Chapter Four

Emory

"Nineteen," I say and burst out laughing as he falls back on the table and with his fingers speared through his hair.

"I'm a dirty old man," He groans like he's in pain and I can't help but laugh louder.

"What are you? Twenty-three?" I roll over and prop myself up on my elbow to look at him lying next to me. "It's not that big of a difference."

He groans again, the sound muffled against his hands as he covers his face. When he finally looks at me, his expression is equal parts amused, intrigued, and horrified. It's really cute.

"Emory. You're fucking hot. How did you get out of Dutton Tennessee a virgin? Didn't you have a boyfriend?"

"I did have a boyfriend. A perfectly nice boyfriend named Eric who was the wide receiver on the football team," I say.

"And he never took you out to the river or the hill or a barn loft or wherever kids go in that town and talk you out of your clothes? Was it a religion thing?"

"We got naked plenty in the back seat of his car. There's lots you can do to have a good time that isn't intercourse, you know."

"I'm aware," he smirks.

"I'm sure you are, smartass. I am *very certain* that there is no sexual activity you haven't tried."

"I draw the line at animals and anything that requires me to get tied up," he says and I can't help but snort with laughter.

23

"Thanks for over-sharing."

"Hey! We're discussing the fact that you're still a virgin at nineteen and that you used to give your boyfriend blow jobs after the game on Friday night but *my* aversion to rope is a problem?"

I stare at him and suddenly realize that this entire conversation is crazy. Zane apparently has the same realization and we bust out laughing like a couple of crazy people. I reach out and snag his hand, giving it a squeeze and taking his guitar pick with me when I retreat. I flip the small metal triangle over my fingers as I try to remember what we were talking about before it became all about my current status as the "Big V".

"To answer your question, it wasn't a religious thing and I'm not saving myself for marriage. I liked Eric and he was hot but I always felt like if I had sex with him then I'd never leave. And I *really needed* to get out of Dutton. I never fit in there." I sigh, feeling the heavy weight of being back in that town settling on my shoulders. I shake it off and let the glorious sun of this afternoon warm my skin instead. "And I was bored and that is *so much worse* than being unhappy."

"Amen" He nods in agreement, his grin making me smile even wider. I like talking to him. A lot. He's refreshingly...blunt.

"So, are you from Nashville?" I ask.

"Nope. Ivy, North Carolina," he says with a grin. "I left the day after high school graduation with a music scholarship to Nashville University and eight hundred dollars in my checking account. I completely get your exodus from Dutton."

"Did your parents freak out too?"

"Oh fuck. It was more like an explosion. I had a huge fight with my dad about my chasing a "dumbass dream" and not staying back in town to work the farm or take a shift at the Goodyear plant. It's the last time we really talked, actually. I don't go home much and they've never been to one of my shows."

He looks down and shrugs and I know that movement. It tries to cover up just how shitty the situation really is and how much it hurts. I am really good at that shrug and I know that it never really helps.

"My mama still cries every time I call home. It breaks my heart but I couldn't stay and I can't go back. Nothing about that place was right after I found out about my daddy." I reach over and touch my guitar, running my fingers lightly over the strings and try to focus on what he was to me before the lie was discovered. As much as he makes me mad, I need to remember my father as a good man. A man who was desperate to find some happiness.

I sit up, picking it up and lightly strumming with Zane's pick.

"How's that going? You and Kit doing okay with all of it?"

I nod, continuing my light strumming. "She's great. The best thing we did was not let what daddy did mess up what we can have together. It wasn't our fault."

"That sounds very healthy."

"Ha! Our joint therapist would disagree." I start playing the chorus of one of my favorite Bob Marley songs and grin when Zane sits up, grabs his instrument and joins in. "We've still got lots of anger and shit but we're trying not to take it out on each other. Some days are easier than others. The close quarters on the tour bus make it interesting."

"How do you feel about your dad?"

"He was very unhappy. Tied to a wife who was mentally ill and a drug addict with a little girl to raise all by himself. He made hurtful, shitty choices but he was just trying to be happy. I have to believe that he didn't mean to hurt anyone."

"It still hurts though, right?"

"All the time."

We play for a few more minutes and then, as if on cue we both roll into a second chorus of "Three Little Birds" by Bob Marley and start to sing. Zane adds this really sweet finger picking thing to the end and we end laughing and singing with really awful Jamaican accents as the song concludes on a messy clash of chords. It isn't pretty but it's fun.

"Bob Marley? You like that song?" He asks, moving right into another tune that I don't know. I listen to the melody, closing my eyes to feel the rhythm. It pulses, a driving undercurrent keeps it edgy and off the pop song spectrum. Not traditional country either but the roots are there. I like it.

"'Three Little Birds' song is a favorite of mine. My daddy gave me this guitar when I was ten years old and he taught me how to play when he was home. That song was the first one I taught myself on my own. There was a book at the library that boasted you could teach yourself to play in ten days or something and I wore it out before I finally had to turn it back in. I surprised him the next time he was home."

"That's a great memory," Zane says. "You need to hold on to that one."

I smile as he firms up the new tune and really starts to play. It is even bolder now and I could see myself singing it at the top of lungs in my car.

"I like that," I say, tapping out the beat on the body of my guitar. "It would make a great chorus. Catchy. All you need is the hook of great lyric."

"So help me write one," he says with a smile and wink. "You know you want to."

The gesture is playful but it also has the heat that always seem to simmer between us. I consider him for a moment knowing that spending more time with Zane Wyatt will likely lead to naked time eventually...even it turns out to just be the music.

But he's right. I really want follow this thing wherever it goes. It's why I left Dutton.

I listen to him play for a few moments longer and then when he looks at me with his unanswered question in his eyes, I have the answer for him.

"How about this?" I sing as he plays lightly, adjusting his pacing to my words.

"When I met you, twenty-two /I knew it would be life or death/Love or lies/You and me for now or never."

Zane stops, stares at me and I hold my breath. Do I suck? Will he laugh?

"Well? What do you think?" I ask, unable to wait another second.

"Little Bird, I think it sounds like the start of a great fucking great song."

Chapter Five

Zane

"Zane, I'm not old enough to get in this club."

I look at Emory standing in between me and Mac on the sidewalk staring at the huge bouncer standing at the entrance of the Javelin Club in St, Louis. We just finished the first of our two shows here and we're wired from the adrenaline of a night full of great music and an amazing audience. Emory and I have been working on new songs every spare minute but we need a night off.

And I wanted to do something with Emory away from the bus and the tour. A night so I can see whether this connection growing between us is a product of the tour fishbowl or something purely us.

"I'll get you in," I say with confidence when she gives me a skeptical look. "I know the owner and I called ahead. You can't come to St. Louis and miss music at the Javelin."

I grab her hand and tug her behind me as I head to the door. A quick word with the slab of meat impersonating a man at the door and we are inside. Emory gives me a look of surprise and I stop abruptly, my hand over my heart in mock hurt.

"You doubted me?"

She pokes at my chest and rolls her eyes. "You're a big talker. Sooner or later you're not going to be able to deliver."

I lean in close, bringing our faces nose-to-nose. I can see the flecks of gold in her emerald green eyes and the mischief buried in their depths. I want to close the distance even more and kiss her but I've promised myself that I'm not going to indulge in that particular vice. I'm pretty sure she's as addictive as heroin.

"Little Bird, you wound me with your disbelief."

"I can get you a band-aid," she says, her lips forming a sexy pout. She slides a look at the big guy standing next to us. "Mac will kiss it and make it better."

"You two lovebirds need to keep my lips and any of my shit out of this." Mac grumbles, his teeth flashing white in the dim light when he grins. "But you two should just go ahead and get it over with. I can practically feel the vibration between you."

I wave him off. "That's just the music, Mac."

"You keep telling yourself that asshole." He turns to Emory and taps her under the chin with his finger. "You can do better sweetheart. Just be strong."

She laughs in his face, reaching up on tiptoes to press a kiss to his cheek. "I should fall for you, Mac."

"But you won't. You'll fall for the tattoos and the long hair and he'll convince you that it really is nine inches." He gives her a pitiful look and a mournful shake of his head. His version of the sad puppy vibe that most girls fall for. "It's the story of my life."

Emory looks skeptical, biting her bottom lip looking like she really is considering her options. My chest tightens, just a little, at the thought that she might pick someone else.

Connection. We've got it.

"Come on Little Bird, I don't want you to miss Kirby Grace." I remove her hand from Mac's and lead her down the hallway towards the burble of the crowd.

"Why do you call her that?" Mac asks, as he helps us elbow through the growing mass of people.

I slide my glance over to Emory and smile. She grins back and it's like we share a secret. "She's a Bob Marley fan."

"Well, then you'll love Kirby, Emory," Mac says.

We both use our bodies to protect Emory from the drunks and the gropers that flock to the Javelin on the weekends. It's always busier when Kirby plays. Mac is a big guy so he gets us to the concert area and I scan the crowd for my buddy. I see him in the distance and nod at him. He points his fingers at a spot in the front and I give him a thumbs up.

I motion to the front to Mac and we push through the growing crowd until we reach the prime spot on the rail, right in front of the band. It's going to be standing room only and we have the best "seats" in the house.

"What's so great about this guy?" Emory asks, her voice raised to be heard over the crowd. Her eyes are roving over all the instruments placed on the stage, the traditional ones and the others Kirby has collected during his travels over the years. "I've never heard of him."

"Kirby is a half-Jamaican/half-Korean musician who has created this fusion of sound that is like a mix of George Clinton, the Red Hot Chili Peppers, and the Foo Fighters. I have never heard anyone play anything or arrange anything like he does. He will blow you away."

She looks excited and the spark of interest in her eyes tells me that this was a good idea. I've discovered that we have a lot in common with our backgrounds and personalities but our love of music is something I've never really found with anyone else.

She soaks it in, every type of sound, technique, style. Her iPod is the most schizophrenic blend of genre, era and type of music I've ever seen. There is nothing she won't try just to see if it will work. There is no sound she ignores because of "the rules". There is nothing she won't try to learn. Emory is fearless and it is such a fucking turn-on.

I love the music but I think I forgot how much since I got so wrapped up in the business stuff and my drive to get a contract. Emory has awakened the sleeping beast inside me again and that is dangerous because I can't separate one from another. And that ability to keep sex and music and life and career in their own swim lane is what has kept me on track, kept me sane.

And now I feel like I am certifiable.

The arrival of Kirby and his huge band on the stage

interrupts our discussion. The crowd goes nuts and I know I'm going to be deaf because I've spent the entire night surrounded by ten decibel sound. Mac and will be yelling at each other on the bus for the next twenty-four hours. Occupational hazard.

Kirby wastes no time jumping right into the set and usually I end up watching his performance and soaking in all of his techniques but tonight, I can't stop looking at Em. Her eyes are riveted to the stage, her entire body pulsing to the driving beat of the drums. She's not only hearing it with her ears but I can see her absorbing the sound through her pores. Her eyes flutter closed and I have to swallow hard against the surge of longing that settles in my groin.

I ease up behind her and grip her hips with my hands, encouraging her to move with the music. She doesn't look at me but leans into my touch and soon we are one body moving together. The pace is frantic, Kirby isn't known for playing ballads, and soon we are part of the mass of bodies writhing together on the dance floor as the set rolls from one song to another.

Her skin is slick with sweat where my hands glide along her body, her hair a cloud of gold curls that tease me with every brush and sweep. Time screams by at the speed of an amazing set and when the band takes a break we are breathless and laughing and amped up on adrenaline more powerful than a Redbull high with a Mountain Dew chaser.

I look around for Mac but he's long gone, chasing some cute little brunette, no doubt.

Kirby catches my eye as he's heading off stage and motions towards the back. I nod and spin Emory around, putting my hands on her hips as I guide her through the crowd.

"You want to meet him? I ask.

She twists around to look up, her eyes huge. "You know him?"

"Little Bird, I know everybody worth knowing."

She rolls her eyes and makes the "let's go" motion with

her hand and I steer her through the crowd. We get to the security guy at the entrance to backstage and he mumbles into his Bluetooth headset before stepping aside and letting us through. The sound level is about a million times lower and we both give a sigh of relief.

Kirby and his entire band is in the large dressing room used by the group and he comes over and pulls me into a huge hug. A big man, his multi-colored dread locks and pierced nose and lip give him an edgy look but his smile is warm and open.

"Zane Wyatt." He pulls back to look at me with an eyebrow raised. "You up to no good?"

I laugh. "Same shit, different day." I turn and introduce him. "Kirby, this is Emory Cabell."

She sticks her hand out but he waves it off and pulls her into a hug. "Nice to meet you Emory." He pauses when he releases her and gets a good look. "You look familiar. Aren't you Kit's long-lost little sister?"

She nods, her excitement from being recognized in the flash of her eyes. "I am. Do you know her?"

"I have met her twice. Very talented young woman." He smiles and grabs her hand, testing the fingertips for the telltale callouses. "You are a musician too?"

"She plays guitar like a dream but her voice..." I say and bite my bottom lip in mock ecstasy. "...her voice is like a sultry wet dream, K."

"Well hell, then I want to hear you."

"I hope you will someday," Emory says, the pink of her blush making her pink cheeks brighter than they were from the dancing. "How do you know Zane?"

I groan, knowing he's going to spill the beans. He loves to tell the story. She picks up on my distress and reaches out to grab Kirby's hand and squeeze.

"He looks like he's about to throw up. Now you've got to tell me."

He doesn't even hesitate. Bastard. "We were both playing a music festival in..." He looks at me with a question.

"...Chicago?"

"Seattle," I correct him and settle back to wait for the bus he's driving to run over me.

"Right, Seattle. They had all of the acts staying at the same motel and at about three in the morning I hear someone knocking hard on my door. I get up to see what's going on and I get a full view of Zane Wyatt standing in the hallway with not a stitch of clothing on and his junk flying around like it was a free-range chicken."

"Are you kidding?" Emory chuckles, her hand coming up to cover her mouth when I glare at her for laughing at me.

"No, but that's not the best part of it." Kirby wheezes with the force of his own laughter and wipes at his eyes. "Apparently he'd had an overnight guest with him and had picked up condoms from one of the vendors at the festival."

"Glow-in-the-dark condoms," I mutter under my breath.

"Oh yeah. Day-glo orange, glow-in-the-dark condoms from some crunchy, tarot-card reading chick who also sold love potions and alien shaped butt plugs." He leans over and mock whispers to her. "I would never have bought anything from that chick. She was crazy."

"And cheap," I add.

"And cheap." He agrees with a firm nod of his head and continues. "Because whatever cut-rate rubber she bought was not colorfast and Zane's frank and beans were stained day-glo orange." He gave me a wink. "And while his cock is mighty impressive it looked like an inverted roadwork cone."

"Thank you," I say because you should always thank someone who complements your junk.

"You're welcome but that color was hideous. You looked like a exhibitionist Ooompa Loompa trying to escape from a porno," he says and then breaks down into fits of laughter that have him bowled over and trying to catch his breath.

Emory gives me a look of disbelief and then joins him as they snort, giggle, and crack-up for several minutes while I wait patiently for them to get control of themselves. When they wind down I flip Kirby the bird.

"Fuck you, man. Why do you always have to tell that stry?"

"I'm glad he spilled it," Emory says and gives him a high five.

"Of course you are."

"Oh baby," she croons and loops her arm around my neck and kisses my cheek. I tighten my hold on her and let my hands enjoy a little bit of exploration along her warm back. "Are your feelings hurt?"

"A little." I pout and try to gain some sympathy points and keep her pressed against me a little while longer. I am not above taking advantage to cop a feel. My cock is half-hard between us and when I shift out position to get a better grip on her, it presses into her belly. Her eyes flare for just a second and she grinds back. Just a little. If I wasn't so focused on her, I would have missed it.

"I'll make it up to you," Kirby says, his gaze telling me that he didn't miss anything that just happened. "You guys need to join me in a song during the next set."

"Really?" Emory gasps, her eyes wide. "I would love that."

Kirby laughs and points to a binder lying on the coffee table. "There's the set list. You go pick out which one you want to do with us."

She lets go of me and I suppress my disappointment. Kirby watches her for a moment as she flips the pages and then returns his gaze to me.

"So, what's with the kid? You never bring women to my show with you."

"She's nineteen, K," I say and note the defensiveness in my tone.

"I'm not going to arrest you, I'm only asking."

"We're writing songs together." Answering a question he never even asked.

"Is that what you're calling it these days?" He glances

back over her where she is happily discussing songs with his drummer, Gonzo. "Does she know that you trade-in writing partners like some people switch their shoes? Because, I gotta tell that she's into you."

He isn't telling me anything I don't already know. But he doesn't know what I'm about to say.

"It's mutual."

He swings back to look at me, his dark brown eyes wide. "I know you want to fuck her but that sounded like something more than that."

"It is." I pause and gather my thoughts. "I don't know. It's never been like this for me. She fascinates me. Everything about her makes me sit up and take a gazillion notes. It's intense between us."

"It could just be the music," he says, his tone neutral.

"It could." And that is all I want to say or get to say because his break is over and Emory is back with her song choice.

On stage the crowd is incredible. In a place this small, you can see their faces, feel the body heat even more than the lights above us, and you can feel the vibration of people getting off on the music all over the place.

Unlike on stage with Kit, Emory and I are side-by-side and as we perform our bodies touch and glide against each other.

She chose *Cherry Bomb* by The Runaways and I am blown away as her sexy, raw voice just tears it up and has the crowd going wild. The song is perfect for her. Suggestive lyrics about a wild-eyed teenage sex kitten living next door in boring-ass suburbia. She slithers to the edge of the stage and entices all the men in the room to enter the fantasy of them popping her cherry and pissing off all the women who have reason to doubt their men.

It's the kind of performance most people would kill to deliver and she nails it. I don't know what Emory's plans are in the music business but if she wants to be huge, she only has to keep doing what she's doing.

Kirby catches my eye across the stage and mouths "wow" when she hits the first chorus on her knees, crotch open in mock invitation.

There isn't a man in a five-mile radius who wouldn't pop a boner like the one I have in my jeans right now, hidden behind my guitar. My mouth goes dry and I have to clear my throat to offer any kind of limited harmony as she stands up and dives into the second verse. I can't take my eyes off her or my mind from picturing her backstage, against a wall with my cock buried deep.

Fuck.

As if she can read my mind, Emory turns the heat on me and makes eye contact as she vibrates and gyrates to the beat. She inches closer, increasing the tension and the heat between us with each step. She gets close to me and slides up and down, using my body like a stripper pole and the crowd echoes the roar in my head by going fucking nuts at the show.

I watch her and she keeps her eyes on me so I don't see it coming when her hand sneaks to my package and gives it a squeeze to emphasize the same scenario in the lyrics. I buck up into her hand, involuntarily, and growl with my own frustration and need. She's playing with fire and from the slow blink she levels at me and the curl of her lips around the last chorus, she's not worried about getting burned.

Holy hell.

The song ends in a raucous avalanche of sound but I can barely hear it over the pounding of my own blood in my ears.

She's right there. Smiling. Laughing. Eyes full of emerald fire. Hair damp and her exposed skin glistening with her sweat.

I kiss her.

There is no way I'm not going to kiss her right now.

I wrap my arm around her waist, push my guitar to the side and pull her tight against me. I spear the fingers on my free hand into her hair and tug on it, forcing her face up so that I can take her mouth. I dive in, tongue thrusting inside her wet heat and it's only a matter of seconds before she's right there with me and it's nothing but mouths and tongues and wet, dark fire.

It goes on and on. Or maybe for just a few seconds. All I know is that time fucking stops.

I break it off and lick my lips, dipping my head down close enough to say in her ear. "That was *not* the fucking music."

Chapter Six

Emory

Performing on stage is amazing but I think I love jamming with the guys even more.

Kit says that people are either born performers, like Zane, or someone who learns how to do it. I am definitely in the second group and I know how lucky I am to get to tour with this amazing group of people and watch them do it right, show after show. I'm getting the hang of it but I feel like I really hit my groove when it's just a bunch of people sitting around and playing our favorite songs, both old and new.

Like right now. We have a show tonight but we're packing up and leaving on the buses as soon as it's over in order to hit the road and make the next city. So, no hotel rooms for us but lots of downtime at the stadium in between the PR stuff, sound check, and show time. So Kit surprised us all with a cookout in the parking lot. Ribs, BBQ chicken and enough baked beans, coleslaw, and corn-on-the-cob to choke a horse, spread out before us by the catering company she hired.

Now the food is gone and we are all so full that all we can do is sit around in a circle in the afternoon sunshine and play music. I grabbed a spot on a small hill of grass in between Zane and Mac and now I'm watching and learning from the more experienced musicians. I add my guitar and my voice to the mix when I can.

Country. Rock. Folk. You name and we've played it, jumping from Jerry Lee Lewis to Green Day to Miley Cyrus in the span of a few chord progressions. When the bass player,

Aaron, starts to play *Freebird* everyone groans and throws empty soda and beer cans at him until he stops with a loud "fuck you" aimed at all of us.

"He's such an asshat," Mac says, his smile softening the blow in his words. These guys are like a family right down to the pranks and the constant taunts. "Nobody really likes that fucking song unless there are shots involved."

"Sometimes you guys make me glad that I'm an only child," I joke.

Zane nudges me with an elbow. "You *were* an only child. You've got a big sister now to boss you around, steal your diary and put Nair in your shampoo bottle."

"Do sisters really do that to each other?" I ask, shuddering when they both nod. Now I'm really thankful Kit and I didn't grow up together. "Well, then I better start locking up my make-up bag on the bus."

"You guys should play that song you were working on the other day. It is so ready primetime," Mac says, his abrupt change of subject catching me off guard.

I shake my head. "It really isn't."

I look at Zane for support and I'm not thrilled by the mischief in his dark eyes.

"I knew you'd say that. This is my 'not shocked' face," Mac says at the same time he signals to Kit and points at me and then Zane. "Zane and Emory have a new song they want to sing."

"We do not!" I punch Mac in the arm, the embarrassment from suddenly being the center of everyone's attention adding extra heat to my sun-drenched skin.

"Come on Little Bird. You did great at Kirby's show. This is just the same thing but with your own song." Zane's voice, low and husky tickles my ear as he leans in close. I lean into it, relishing the closeness and recalling last night and the kiss onstage. He's a touchy guy, unafraid to put his hands on me if he feels like it. I love it and I find myself wishing he would do it more often. He also uses it to shamelessly press his advantage. "Just say yes. This is what you left home to do."

I groan and dip my head as the crowd around us starts doing that chant thing, rounds of "sing, sing" punctuated by guitar strums and laughter.

"Em! Zane!" Kits yells out over the noise and I look up to meet her eyes. She gives us the "go ahead" gesture and I know I'm giving in. Apparently everyone else does too because the chant becomes cheers and Zane chuckles beside me. Bastard.

"This is gonna be so good," he says, his fingers poised over his guitar as he flashes me a triumphant smile. I let my eyes roam over his face for a moment, the memory of how soft his goatee was against my skin when he kissed me making me shiver a little. "You ready?"

I nod and listen for his soft count as we both launch into the driving beat and Zane takes the first half of the first verse.

When I met you, twenty-two, blown away by the fire in your eyes/You took my hand and led me into the night/the sparks between us the only light/I knew it would be life or death/Love or lies/You and me for now or never.

My turn comes and for a split second the butterflies have a free fall in my stomach but Zane's smile makes me bold. I open my mouth and I sing like my next breath depends on it.

When I met you/twenty-two/in love with the fire in your eyes/Your hand in mine was my lifeline, my spark/Your touch the kick start to my heart/ Reckless/Fearless/Love or lies/You and me now or never

By the time we hit the chorus the band is picking out their parts and playing along. When we get to the bridge the entire thing explodes in a wall of sound that makes me laugh with the pure joy of it. Zane is right, music is seductive and addictive. I could do this forever. I hope I will.

I look at him as we launch into the last chorus and the connection between us ignites, rivaling the summer sun in its intensity. Our voices blend in perfect, edgy harmony, sliding together as if they were made for each other. Zane's gaze is onyx, backlit with a copper fire and the "I-told-you-so" smile on his lips is pure seduction. I want nothing more to lean over and take his mouth as we drive through the last few notes.

My heart is pounding in my head and my chest so loudly that I don't notice that the entire area has gone silent for a few seconds. Zane reaches out and wraps his big hand around the back of my neck, drawing me to him with sexy intent in his eyes. Just like that, I'm back on the stage at the Javelin and I want him to kiss me again. I need him to kiss me. I lean in, licking my lips and ready to taste him again when the area around us erupts in applause. We both jerk at the sound but instead of pulling away immediately, he touches our foreheads together for the briefest second.

He holds me there long enough for him to growl in a voice just loud enough for me to hear, "That *wasn't* just the music." And then he's dragging me to my feet and I'm dazed, nodding thanks to everyone who clearly loved the song.

"Holy shit you guys!" Kit is on her feet, her face pink with her excitement. She makes her way over to us and crushes me in a hug as tight as a guitar still strapped to my body will allow. She lets me go and squeezes Zane too. "That was a crazy good song. You two are amazing together and I want you to play that one during my second costume change. I've been looking for something to put there to maintain the high energy of the set and that song would be perfect. You'll do it, yeah?"

I just blink at her, unable to process what she's saying to us. I know I sound as shell-shocked as I feel when I finally speak.

"On stage? During the show?"

"Yes, during the show. You've got to know how awesome that song really is." She turns to Zane and pokes him in the gut. "*You* know how good that song is."

He nods, smirking and not even trying to hide his ego. "It's a fucking Top Ten song, Kit. Too bad you can't sing it as a solo."

I expect her to balk at this but she nods in agreement. "It's absolutely a duet. It's like Johnny and June and Tammy and George and Faith and Tim all had an orgy and a song baby popped out of a cake at the end."

I laugh. She's right. I never would have thought to put it that way but she's right.

"You should find someone to cut the single with," I add, knowing she could have a huge hit on her hands with this one.

She looks us both over, her eyes betraying that she has some kind of calculation going on in her head. I know she won't share with the class until she's ready but I would bet money that she has plans for that song. I let my own head get a little bigger when I realize that I'm one-half of the team that wrote it.

"I really want you guys to perform it during the show. Not tonight. Tomorrow. You'll have time to rehearse it with the band. Will you do it?" She asks, giving me the wide-eyed look that tells me she will keep asking until I say yes. I may not have known her long, but Kit is like a terrier when she gets her mind set on something. It's one of the many reasons she is such a huge success.

I look at Zane and suddenly all of the elation I felt minutes before melts into a huge case of nerves.

"You can do this." Zane says, his hand reaching out to snag my own in a loose tangle of fingers. "I'll be right there with you the whole time."

"This is what I came here to do." I say in reply, feeling the truth of them down in my bones. It's leap-of-faith time, figuring out who I am by leaving no stone and no opportunity untaken. "Right?"

He nods. His eyes dark, solemn and intense on mine.

"Is that a yes?" Kit asks, bouncing up and down on her toes until I nod yes. She pumps her fist in the air and presses a kiss to my cheek. "Excellent. This is going to be great. I know it." Her phone rings and she fishes it out of her pocket, grimacing when she looks at the screen. "I've got an interview in an hour. Off to get all dolled up."

I watch her as she walks away, meeting her personal assistant in the middle of the scattering crowd and then jumping in a golf cart and taking off for the stadium. I feel a tug on my fingers and I shuffle to cover the two steps between me and Zane. He gazes down at me, his smirk less playful and more predatory. Just that one look and my skin flashes hot all over. The sounds around us fade into the background. We might as well be alone here in this parking lot.

He's right. It *isn't* just the music.

He stares at me for a few seconds longer, his expression shielding whatever decision tree he's scaling in his mind. But I don't need him to make this decision for me. I know what I want to do.

Look. Leap. Live.

"Come with me." I tug on his hand and weave my way through the crowd, making a beeline for what I hope is my empty tour bus. Kit is occupied with her makeup and I hope Sandra is busy doing something else for a while.

Zane follows behind me, his hand still clinging to mine and his smartass mouth unusually silent. We cross the lot and reach the bus without any interruption. I open the door and step inside, dragging him behind me. The interior is cool and darker with the window shades pulled shut against the harsh summer sun. I don't hear anyone else here but I need to make sure.

"Sandra?" When no one responds I turn to brush past Zane and lock the door.

I don't even get to turn around before he's pressed along my back, his hands reaching around to slip my guitar over my head. His warmth is gone for the briefest second and I spin around and catch him placing my instrument on the table alongside his own. Zane turns back to around, walks slowly towards me and stops far enough away for me to wish he was closer and near enough that I can feel the heat of afternoon pouring off his skin.

"I want to put my hands all over you," he says and my mouth goes dry. He takes my silence as permission to close the distance between us and do exactly what he said. A whisper of a calloused finger over my collarbone and then the same shiver-inducing touch travels up my neck until his large hands are cradling my face."Em, you say the word and I'll let you go and walk out the door. We can just make great music together and that will be it. Otherwise, I'm not going to stop until I make you come."

I tense the tiniest bit at his words. I try to hide it but he senses it and smiles.

"I won't fuck you here. You deserve better for your first time than the couch on a tour bus. And just because we have some fun today doesn't mean that it ever has to lead to anything else, anything more. You're always in control of this ride, Little Bird."

His words soothe my only worry and I take my immediate future in my hands and close the distance between our mouths.

I gasp at the first touch. He's surprisingly gentle this time, completely different from the kiss in the club. Zane's tongue pushes past my lips and teases me, entices me to take what I want. So I do.

I grab his shirt and drag him closer, pressing our mouths together in a clash of teeth and tongues and hot, wet possession. He groans, his fingers twisting in my hair and setting off sparks of almost-pain behind my eyelids. I dig my nails into the hard muscle of his shoulders, hungry to have him all over me as soon as possible.

Zane maneuvers us around until the edge of the couch hits the back of my knees. He breaks off the kiss and lowers me to the cushioned seat. He remains standing, looking down at me with eyes dark and hot, his lips swollen from our kiss. Our breathing is harsh and heavy in the silence broken only by his voice, tinged dark with need.

"I've been hard for days." He rubs a hand over the bulge of his cock behind his jeans and my eyes are drawn to that spot and I can't look away. His long fingers trace the length of it, unfastening the top button, then two before dipping inside to shift his erection under the denim until I can see the fat, wet tip over the waistband. Suddenly my mouth is dry as sand. "You keep me hard all the time Emory. I want you so fucking much."

I look up at the edge of pain in his voice. I know it's the good kind of agony, the kind that has kept me up late in my bunk, my own hands touching me while I pretend it is him. But I don't have to pretend anymore. All I have to do is be bold. He's in front of me and he's mine for the taking.

I sit up and slide my palm against the hard length of him, my fingertips tracing the head. I smile when his hips push up against my touch, increasing the pressure on a long, deep groan. His long hair has fallen down, shielding his expression with the bowing of his head and I miss seeing the fire in his eyes. But his body, taut and trembling tells me everything I need to know.

His head snaps up when my fingers begin unbuttoning the rest of the buttons on the fly of his jeans. I'm staring back at him so I fumble as I release one button, then two, then a third until I feel his hot flesh against the palm of my hand. I break eye contact then and watch as I wrap my fingers around his fat, hard dick. I've not had the chance to see many penises up close and personal but I've seen enough to know that he is beautiful.

"Gorgeous, "I breathe out on a whisper as I stroke him from the silken-soft head down to the nest of dark hair around the root.

A flush of heat creeps across my skin, a hint of embarrassment but the look of pure want on his face makes me not care. There is nothing I can do or say in this moment that would be wrong. This is Zane. And while I don't understand our connection, it's there. So, I go for broke and tell him exactly what is on my mind because I know he'll give it to me.

"I want this in my mouth."

Chapter Seven

Zane

There is a good chance I might not survive this.

I've had many women and men. All ages, sizes, hair color. We've used every kind of toy, costume, and mind-fuckery you can imagine. It was all hot, more than enough to get me off but sight of my sweet Emory with her long, slim fingers wrapped around my cock has me about to blow.

"Jesus," I huff out on a sharp exhale, shifting my hips forward to thrust into her grip. "Such dirty talk from a woman who looks like a fucking angel."

"I left my halo back at home," she answers and I chuckle at the stubborn tilt to her jaw. She thinks I'm going to back down from this, that my scruples will keep me from taking what she is offering. I'm a nice guy most of the time but never a saint.

I reach down and grab my dick, tracing the tip along the bottom lip she just licked in conscious or unconscious invitation. I'm not entirely sure if it's too much but she doesn't pull away. Her mouth opens on a moan and the moist heat of her breath along my tight skin makes me grit my teeth with the effort to hold back.

My experience with virgins ended when I popped my cherry in the hayloft with Becky Tanner. It had been a fun time; as much fun as two horny, clueless kids can have with a free afternoon and a stolen box of condoms. Emory says she's has experience in other things so I'll follow her lead until she tells me to stop.

"What does it say about me that I just want to dirty you

up?" I drop to my knees in front of her spreading her thighs with my hands, letting my fingers wander over the silky skin on her inner thigh. I push her skirt up and the vision of the tiny panties barely covering her sex makes my balls tighten. I lift up until I can look in her eyes, loving the flash of gold-tinged desire in their depths. "A fucking angel, that's what you are and my idea of heaven is your lips wrapped around my cock."

She bites her lower lip, her hands sliding under my t-shirt to stroke my side, my abdomen. I arch into her touch at the same time I lean forward and kiss her. Slow and deep, coaxing and deliberate. I don't need to ravage her; she's right here with me and ready to explore how good this can be. Emory wants this, every touch, every sigh tells me loud and clear.

After weeks of slow burn we are ready to catch fire.

I pull back from the allure of her mouth and sit on my heels, my dick dragging along the exposed flesh of her thigh, enticing me to maintain the contact, to grind against her. But I want her to get off first. We don't have tons of time and I need to show her how good I can make her feel.

I hook fingers on the waistband of her panties and drag them down her legs and toss them somewhere behind me. She spreads her legs wider and it's my turn to groan at the display. Pale skin, the darker pink of her pussy, and blonde trimmed curls.

"You're gorgeous," I whisper, glancing to find her watching me. I smile at her and she gives one back to me, a little shy but full of anticipation. I won't make her wait. I run my palms against her inner thigh, spreading her wider to make room for my shoulders as I dip my head and take the first taste.

A long slow glide of tongue along her pussy lips, already slick with her own arousal. It is a sweet and sharp burst on my taste buds and I fight the urge to reach down and stroke myself. Instead I spread her open, allowing me to lick and suck and kiss every perfect inch of her.

Emory pushes against my face, her breathing harsh and

staccato in the silence of the tour bus. This is going to go fast. We've been riding this edge of arousal for weeks and going over is a like a landslide: quick, dirty, and destructive. Whatever walls we put up between us will be rubble after today.

"Zane," she says on a gasp and I glance to see her squeezing her breasts, her tank top rucked up and exposing the tender expanse of her belly. She's biting her lip as her fingers slip inside of her bra and begin a slow rub against a nipple. I would give my right nut to get rid of her clothes and see her play with the taut flesh but I don't want to stop what we are doing for the time it would take to get everything off.

I lower my head and deliver a hungry kiss to her sex, finding her clit and passing the tip of my tongue over it in a rapid rhythm calculated to make her scream my name. Her body is hot and wet against my finger as I push it inside her, loving the way her muscles draw me in deeper. Her hips are bucking under me and I use my other hand to grasp her hip and hold her in place.

She makes a sound, something between a whine and a plea when I add another finger and start pumping inside her. I finger fuck her, wishing that I could do it with my cock buried deep inside her.

Not today. Not here.

"Zane!" Her cry is rough and ragged as she shudders against me, her hand grabbing my shoulder and digging in with her nails as she comes all over my tongue. I continue my kiss, licking and caressing until she relaxes against me, her breathing rapid but deep.

I look up at her, her cheeks flushed a bright pink and her breasts heaving up and down with her gulping inhale and exhale. It's her eyes that capture me, dark forest green and open, soft, eager.

"Come here," she whispers as she tugs on my shoulder, encouraging me to join her on the couch.

I'm happy to oblige, lifting up with a plan to kiss her but I'm distracted by the nipple peeking over the edge of her bra cup. I lower my head and lick the flesh, loving her gasp and the way she arches into my touch, begging for more. I pull aside the soft fabric and continue my tongue lashing until the deep pink skin is shiny with my attention.

"God, that's pretty," I murmur as I reach around her back and under her top to unclasp the bra. With the tension gone, I pull down the other cup and bow my head to swirl my tongue around that nipple until it is hard and straining against my lips. That one is also pretty and I know I could spend hours feasting in the tips, the soft mounds of her breasts.

"Kiss me," Emory begs as she writhes under me, her fingers exploring every inch of me she can reach under my clothes. Her touch lights me up and them leaves me colder and hungrier when she moves to another spot. I reach over my head and pull my t-shirt off and then lean up to let my moan mingle with her own when my bare flesh connects with hers. "Kiss me, Zane. I want to know what I taste like on your mouth."

My plan to make the kiss slow and seductive goes out the window at her dirty plea. This meeting of our mouths is hard and bruising as I lose a little bit of my control. In the back of head I know we'll both bear marks from the ferocity of our kiss but I don't care. I plunge my tongue inside and make sure she can taste every drop of her passion.

"Your juice is sweet, salty. I could eat you all fucking day," I say against her lips, before I delve back in for another tour of her wet heat. Her hands are all over me and I jerk forward when the warmth of her palm wraps around my dick and squeezes. I pull away with a gasp.

"Come on, I want to taste you. Bring it up here," she asks while urging me up on the couch with the hand not driving me crazy.

I put a knee on each side of her body, hovering over her with the perfect angle to watch her lean forward and take my cock inside her perfect mouth.

"Fuck," I grind out, my eyes shut tight against the electrifyingly sensation of being covered by her hot, wet suction. Emory and her little high school boyfriend might not have gotten all the way to home base but she spent a lot of time practicing the art of polishing his nob at third. "Oh fuck."

My knees go a little weak, so I pitch forward and loom over her, my hands braced against the back of the couch. I pry my eyes open and I realize that this is the best fucking seat in the house. The scene before me is dirty and debauched and I will never get it out of my head, never.

My jeans are shoved down to mid-thigh, my dick sliding in between her lush, pink lips and her eyes are on mine, making sure I know how much she loves this. I throw out any worry that she can't handle me and I let my usual pervy, freak flag fly.

"Fucking gorgeous mouth all over me. Suck me off, baby." I gasp as I reach down and grip my shaft with hand, holding it out to her so she can take all of me. She moans deep in her throat and slides me all the way in and I can feel the vibration in my balls. It is so fucking sweet. I have to grit my teeth as I begin a slow pulse of my hips. "You feel so good, Em. So damn beautiful. Made for me."

I'm almost babbling and I know it but she loves it, her fingernails digging into my bare ass and hip as I speed up with my thrusts. I'm so close and I know there is no way I'm going to make it last. She's so amazing, so giving and I can't believe how she exceeds every single fantasy I ever had about this moment.

Emory Cabell is perfect and I know that this afternoon will not be enough. I hope she's ready for me because I don't think I'll be able to stay away from her.

She shudders underneath me and I glance down in time to see her lower her hand in between her own legs. Any direct view of what she's doing is blocked by my body and her skirt but the knowledge that going down on me has turned her on so much that she needs to touch herself sets me off like a firecracker.

"I'm going to come." I give her the warning and I ease

back a little, giving her the choice on whether she wants to swallow or not. She chases my retreat and I have my answer and nothing stands between me and the pleasure pain of my orgasm. I grip the back of the couch tightly as it hits me like a tsunami, wave after wave making me shudder and twitch and writhe against the sensation.

I pull out of her mouth and slither down the couch until we are face-to-face and breathing like we both just ran a marathon. I kiss her, letting it linger and enjoying the heat of our bodies where we touch. Emory writhes against me, her hips moving in the unmistakable rhythm of someone who is still on the edge. I remember her hand under her skirt and I pull back just enough to murmur against her lips.

"You still need me, baby?" When she nods yes, I wedge my own hand between us and find her wet and swollen between her legs. I stroke her gently, somewhere between a tease and what she needs as I explore her soft skin with my lips. Nuzzling my nose along her cheek and behind her ear until I am surrounded by citrus spice of her shampoo. She comes against my hand, more gently than before and I return to her mouth, soaking in her gasp of pleasure.

Holy shit. She's perfect.

I tell her so and she just laughs at me. I do not have the strength to argue with her.

I wrap her up in my arms and maneuver us until we are able to lie together on the couch, legs woven in a complicated puzzle. We doze there for a while, enjoying the silence and each other until I can hear other people coming back to the tour buses to grab whatever shit they need to take to the dressing rooms to get ready for the show. I check my watch and groan.

"I don't want to move but we've got get moving or we'll be late," I say, lifting up to look down at her. Her hair is a wreck, her lips dark pink and swollen and her clothes look like she's been mauled by a bear. I grin. "You look amazing."

"I look like I just came twice on a couch during an afternoon booty call." She sits up, stretching her arms and reaching behind her to refasten her bra. I would offer to help but she looks so damn cute when her face screws up in frustration. When she finally gets it done, she catches me staring. "What?"

I shrug. "Is this a one-and-done or are you up another round on another afternoon?" I smile. "Or night?" I smile wider. "Or morning?"

She shoves against my shoulder and laughs but I can see the pink blush on her cheeks. There's the Emory I know and can't wait to get my hands on again.

"I could do that," she says and shoves off the couch, looking for her shoes. I can tell she's working hard to play it cool and I follow her lead.

"Well, you check your calendar and let me know," I tease, buttoning up my shorts and grabbing my shoes. "I had fun and I would love to do it again."

"Me too," she says and then pauses, concern looking very out of place on her face. "But we need to try to keep this quiet. I'm not embarrassed but I'm not sure I want everyone in my business."

"You got it."

"Kit won't be surprised."

"No one is going to be surprised, Emory." When she raises and eyebrow, I explain. "We've got heat between us. People already figured that out and they all assume that we'll do something about it. Half of the crew probably thought we were fucking instead writing songs until they heard the one today."

"Of course they did," she laughs and melts against me when I draw her closer. "You *are* Zane Wyatt."

"And you're hot." I press a soft kiss to her lips and then pull back with a sigh when I hear Mac yelling across the parking lot. "Gotta go, Little Bird."

I release her, grab my guitar and follow her to the door. We swing it open and both of us jump back when Billy, one of the roadies, is standing on the step, his big paw wrapped around the arm of a guy with broad shoulders, blonde hair, and a smile only for Emory.

"Eric?" She asks, her mouth hanging open in shock.

"You know this guy, Emory?" Billy inquires, his bored expression screaming just how much he doesn't want to have to deal with this situation. "He says he's your boyfriend."

Chapter Eight

Emory

"Eric, why are you here?"

I'm beat from the show and the last thing I want to deal with is my ex-boyfriend trying to convince me to come home and back to him. Apparently my mom sent him. He's been at me about it since he arrived just before the show and followed me around backstage. Kit offered him a ticket and ignored my glare when he accepted. He seemed to have a good time but I couldn't care less.

All I can think about was the blank glance Zane gave me whenever we came in contact since Eric arrived. Yes, he was polite and friendly and welcomed Eric to the show. He gave him a short tour of the backstage when Kit requested so that I could sneak off and get dressed but I could tell that it was the last thing he wanted to do.

I can't tell if he's pissed or jealous. If I had to guess, it is the first one because there is no way Zane Wyatt is jealous of my old boyfriend. Yeah, our sex session on the couch was amazing but it wasn't a proposal for marriage. There is no reason for either of us to be jealous.

But I know that if I had one of Zane's old bed partners show up, I would definitely have a little green monster sitting on my shoulder.

It's stupid and childish but I know I have a little bit of a crush on him. He's hot and funny and a musician. He has long hair and tattoos and is sex-on-a-stick. I am obligated to have a crush on him. I'm sure there's a law somewhere.

He's also my friend and I love the way he makes me feel.

Not just when his tongue is buried between my legs…but all the time. I feel special when he looks at me.

I know. It's stupid.

But what is dumber is the fact that Eric cannot get the memo and go home.

"Eric, I'm not going home and we are over," I say for the millionth time as we stand outside the door of my tour bus. We leave in fifteen minutes and I was hoping that I would get to see Zane before we get on the road but I can't get rid of my uninvited guest. "You need to go and move on. I'm not coming back to Dutton except to visit my mom."

"Your mom misses you," he says, walking forward until I have to back up and lean against the side of the bus to avoid him. He raises an arm and semi-brackets me in. I used to love this when he did it in high school but right now it's just irritating me with its creeper vibe.

"I miss her too but she'll learn to deal with it. Most parents have to get used to their kids moving out and having their own lives."

"But you left so quickly. One day you were there and the next you were headed to Nashville. It was very sudden."

I laugh and wonder how he knew me so little even with all the time we spent together.

"The only reason you were surprised about me leaving is because you weren't listening. All I ever talked about was going to Nashville to pursue my music."

"That's just stuff people say, Emory." He chuckles and shakes his head and I want to smack him.

Suddenly I'm exhausted and disgusted with him and this conversation. I close my eyes and lean my head back against the cool, metal side of the bus which is why I don't see him make his move.

His mouth on mine isn't unpleasant. Eric is a good kisser and a generous lover. He made sure we both came and always paid for our dates. He's a nice guy, handsome and sexy. I liked him. I like him. I just don't want his tongue down my throat anymore.

I push against his chest and twist my face to the side. Eric pulls back, confusion all over his face as he tries to figure out why I stopped.

"Goodbye Eric. I hope you love college and that you are a huge success and I'll see you when I visit my mom." He opens his mouth to say something and I clarify my comment. "As a friend. We can grab a coffee or something." I pat his chest and duck under his arm to head into the bus. "Drive safely home."

I turn to add a smile to my goodbye when I see Zane standing a few feet away, near the door of his own bus. Mac is beside him, watching the scene closely. I raise my hand to wave Zane over, anxious to talk to him before we hit the road for the night but he just nods and mounts the steps to his bus and disappears. Mac looks at him and then back at me, eyes rolling in a "what the fuck" gesture before he follows in Zane's footsteps.

"Oh shit," I say, slumping against the doorframe. I know Zane saw Eric kiss me and I cringe. It's ridiculous but it feels like cheating. I groan again, realizing just how complicated my life just got.

And then Eric chimes in with the understatement of the century. "That Zane guy is nothing but trouble."

No shit.

***

Zane

"You're ass hurt and you need to get over it."

I flip the bird to the general direction where Mac is standing in the dressing room we share backstage. It's a few minutes to show time and I really don't need him to psychoanalyze me right now.

"Fuck off, Dr. Phil." I pull on my boots and straighten up, rolling my shoulders to ease the tension. "Emory and I were just fooling around. I don't give a shit about this guy showing up. That's her problem to deal with."

"Except that you're a jealous motherfucker who has been a dick all day long to everyone," Mac says with a growl.

"When I have to deal with your bullshit, then it becomes my problem."

I stop what I'm doing and sigh. I know he's right. I have been an asshole all day. Short-tempered and anxious.

"I don't like feeling this way." I offer as an explanation and an apology.

"Jealous? Welcome to the world the rest of us live in."

I sigh and sit down in the makeup chair in front of the vanity. I wish Mateo were here right now. He knows me so well that I wouldn't have to explain but he's across the country and he's got a huge set of medical school exams this week, so I'm not going to call him. He'd just try to fix it. He's hard-wired to save the world.

"I don't like the reason why I feel jealous. I like her, of course, I do. I try to like all the people I hook-up with but I've never felt like I wanted to jack-up some dude for kissing them."

"She wasn't kissing him back. You could tell that from a mile away."

"Yeah, I saw that too."

"It doesn't help?" He asks, wrapping tape around his drumsticks and testing the weight in his hands. "I saw how she looked at you. If you'd been the one with his tongue down her throat, Emory would have been climbing you like a tree."

I remember her under me on the couch, her lips wrapped around my cock. The look in her eyes when I kissed her as she came the second time. I think of that and I know he's right.

"I just need to talk to her," I grumble as we head to door as a roadie gives us the "ten minute" knock on the doorframe. "I hardly saw her all day between interviews and the fan club thing. I'll see if I can grab some time after the show."

"You'll need to make it quick. We're driving all night again."

"I know." I love the road but when we have several "in-and-outs" in a row like this, it becomes grueling. I have to check the calendar to see what city we are in since have no time to explore.

We round the corner and the entire band is there, huddled for the prayer before we hit the stage. Kit is in the middle, her smile lighting up the dim space. She's an incredible performer, a fantastic boss and everyone loves her. The road is hard but she tries to make it fun and feel like a family. Once again I throw up a thank you to the Big Guy for landing me this gig.

Emory and Sandra move up beside me and my eyes are immediately drawn to hers. The emerald green is cloudy with confusion and I hate the fact that I was the asshole that put it there. I reach out and brush my hand against hers, our fingers intertwining for the briefest few seconds before Kit breaks the huddle and we all start to hustle towards the stage.

I take two steps forward and then turn, dragging her to me for a quick but thorough kiss that leaves us both breathless and the taste of her lip gloss on my mouth.

"I'm a dick," I say and she bursts out laughing, leaning up to kiss my cheek before she heads out onto the stage. I follow with a grin on my face for the first time today.

The show goes quickly for me until the point where Emory and I perform *Lies and Love* during the costume change. Out there under the lights, flirting while we sing the words we wrote together, the entire world slows down to a crawl and we are the last two people on it for the final ride. I could have stayed on stage in that moment all night long.

The audience loved it and went nuts, as Kit predicted. The rest of the show was a blur of music, lights, people, and my fingers itching for the chance to touch Emory.

I make it just offstage before I catch up with her and pull her into my arms. This time the kiss is long and deep and borderline indecent. Our bodies, damp with sweat and juiced from the adrenaline of performance writhe against each other. My hands are in her hair, down her back, cupping her ass and hauling her higher against me until she wraps her legs around my waist.

She huffs out a muffled grunt when her back hits the

wall but I don't care since it gives us more leverage to grind against each other. Her hands sneak past the waistband on my jeans and I feel her bare palms against the skin of my ass.

"I'm a dick. Sorry." I say when I finally release her mouth and we grin down at each other. She runs a finger across my lips and I kiss the tip.

"That's a shitty apology, Wyatt."

"I'll make it up to you later."

She opens her mouth to answer but the sound of her sister—my boss—behind us cuts off whatever she was going to say.

"Emory why do you have your hands down his pants?"

Chapter Nine

Emory

I can't sleep.

My body is still buzzing after the hot kiss after the show, adrenaline and arousal making it impossible for me relax. Kit and Sandra are wired too and we all sit on the couch in the common area of the tour bus ogling Ryan Reynolds in *The Proposal*, eating microwave popcorn and drinking.

I fidget, drawing my knees up to my chest as I munch mindlessly on the snack. I love this movie but I am barely following along as the memory of Zane's hands on my body refuse to let me go. It isn't like I've never had a guy touch me, Eric and I spent plenty of time figuring out what felt good. But, nothing he ever did turned me on like getting felt up by Zane Wyatt.

Tipping my bottle back, I realize that it's all gone. That will not do.

"Another round?" I ask as I lift myself off the couch, letting my body settle with the gentle sway of the bus under my feet.

"Emory are you even old enough to drink?" Sandra asks as she eyeballs the beer I wave in her face, taking it with a nod of thanks.

I hand off the Orange Crush to Kit, admiring again how she sticks with her sobriety.

"And if I say no?" I inquire, taking another deep swallow of the pale ale as I lower myself back onto the cushions.

"Nothing. I'm not your mama but she's your big sister and I don't want the boss mad at me because I'm contributing to the delinquency of a minor."

"As long as she keeps it on the bus, I don't care," Kit says, reaching out for another handful of popcorn. "I'm more concerned with the kiss she laid on Zane after the show and what her hands were doing down his pants. They look like they'd been there before."

I quickly swallow my beer and wipe at my mouth when some dribbles down my chin.

"Oh, we're talking about that?' Sandra asks, her afro bouncing a little with her excited nod that matches her wide smile. "Excellent because I gotta tell you that I never believed you two were just writing songs together. Everybody knows that Zane Wyatt gets *all the* women horizontal *all the* time. He can't help it."

"I have not been *horizontal* with Zane," I protest, horrified and relieved that we are talking about this. I need advice and that's what big sisters and girlfriends are for. Right? "We have been writing songs and somewhere along the way...well, we ended up semi-horizontal."

"Do you want to sleep with him?" Kit inquires, her voice calm but her eyes wary.

"I know that's where this is headed if we keep up what we're doing," I hedge, not sure why when I know the answer. I want Zane to fuck me. But saying it out loud feels like I would be committing somehow.

"It's headed to him fucking you and from what I've hear it will be amazing and so worth it. But if you think he's the boyfriend-you-take-home-to-mama-type, then you need to keep walking," Sandra says.

"I know that. He's told me from the beginning what he is but I want more of it anyway." Kit groans and slumps back on the couch and I totally understand her reaction. If I were my big sister, I'd move my ass to Montana. "I know how stupid that is. Any smart girl would give him a wide berth unless they can spread their legs without opening their heart even just a little bit. I also know that I'm one big walking heart, ready and available to soak in all the good and vulnerable as well as all of the bad. I don't want to get hurt but I don't think I want to miss out either."

The room is quiet after my little speech and I wait for them to start with the "are you crazy?" talk.

"Just be careful Em," Kit sighs, leaning over to sling an arm over my shoulder. She squeezes me tight, my head automatically finds the perfect spot on her shoulder and we sit there for several long moments. I close my eyes, so grateful to have her in my life. Dad might not have been legit but I can't hate anything that brought her into my life. "I don't want you to get hurt but I don't want you to miss out on living either. Zane isn't a player, he's straight with the people in his bed and I don't think he would deliberately hurt you. But he's told you what he is and what this can be so the best advice I can give you is to believe him."

"You sound like Zane."

"I'm not sure how I feel about that but if it means he's being straight with you, that's all I can ask. You could do a lot worse than have a summer thing with Zane Wyatt."

"And if he does you wrong, Max Butler will kick his ass for you," Sandra adds her smirk telling me that she wouldn't mind a front-row seat at that event. She's a little blood-thirsty.

They settle down to keep watching the movie but I can't do it. I need to go and think and after the third glance from Sandra as I fidget, I excuse myself and go to my bunk.

I slide into bed and pull the long, dark privacy curtain. I'd heard nightmares about sleeping in a bus bunk but I love it. It's kind of like camping with climate control and no bugs. The motion of the bus lulls me to sleep most nights and I crash until my alarm goes off. I grab my phone and put in my earbuds, scrolling down my music until I find my Patty Griffith playlist. I hit play and settle back against my pillow to do some hard thinking.

I like Zane. I can admit that much and I think he likes me, at least as a friend. I know he wants me, would love to fuck me and that sensation is definitely reciprocated. He's sexy and exciting and adventurous. If I left Dutton looking for a wild ride, he would definitely fit the bill.

But I know that my feelings could very quickly slide into something deeper. I could be wrong. I've never had a fling with someone. Never been a fuck buddy. I could be great at it or I could fall...hard.

My phone rings in my earbuds and I jump at the sudden change to the ringtone. I glance at the number and see Zane's name across the screen. I bite my lip against the smile that blooms there and swipe the screen to accept the call.

"Hey," I say, wincing when a loud yell erupts in the background. "What is that?"

"Hang on, the guys are having a Playstation tournament."

I listen as he moves around on his end, the scrapes and grunts making me laugh as he stumbles over all the crap on the floor to get away from the noise. I've been on the bus and it looks like a frat house on meth. I never take my shoes off. Never.

"Okay, I'm back," he says as I hear the noise disappear. "I'm back in the rehearsal space."

Instead of master bedroom space in the back, their bus has a small room where you can go to get away from the noise of the kitchen and TV area and write some music or have a quiet conversation. We've worked back there a couple of times, both of us wedged onto the loveseat built-in across the width of the bus.

"What's going on?" I ask settling deeper into my bunk, trying to steady my pulse. It kicked up into overdrive the minute I heard his voice.

"I wanted to call you and tell you that I'm sorry I was such a dick."

I smile. "That's an excellent apology, Mr. Wyatt. No waffling. Straight to the point."

"Oh, you're going to give me shit about it, aren't you? I say I'm sorry real nice and you bust my ass."

"What are you sorry for exactly," I tease. "'Being a dick' covers a lot of territory."

It gets quiet on the other end of the phone and I hear

him sigh and mutter "fuck me" under his breath. I should let him off the hook but I'm really curious about why he reacted the way he did. If I don't find out for sure, my hopeful romantic side will run wild. I've seen me do it.

"I didn't like that guy's hand being on you. I didn't like the thought that he'd *ever* had his hands on you." His breathing is harsh in my ears and my body reacts to the growl in his voice. "I still had your taste on my lips and the feel of them around my cock and he was there, looking like he had a right to be."

My mouth is suddenly dry, my nipples hard and my sex tightens. I swallow hard so that I can answer him.

"He has no right to touch me. Not anymore." I take a deep breath and take the plunge, offering up the way I see it. I might be wrong, I might be immature but I want Zane to know where my head and my heart are. "You're the only one that has the right to touch. You're the only one I *want* to touch."

The air in my bunk is stifling and I pull the blanket off me and shove it down to the bottom of the bed.

"Goddam Em. You're killing me over here," he says, his voice thick with what I now recognize is his arousal. "Is that what you want? Some kind of claim on me?"

"I don't know how this works, Zane. You enlighten me."

"What do *you* want? Tell me and I'll give it to you if I can."

What are we talking about? Our hearts? Our bodies? The orgasm I want so badly right now? I clench my thighs together to stem the ache that pulses there just from the sound of his voice over the phone.

"I don't know," I answer, too afraid to say what I'm thinking until I've had more time to think about it. At this point in time, my answer isn't a lie. "I don't know."

"What *do* you know?" His voice is deep and low, seductive. He's really good at keeping me tuned in to his every word.

"I know that I love how I feel when you touch me."

"God, so do I. I want your hands on me all the time."

"I want to do more with you." I take a breath and dive in and confess the one thing I know for sure. "I want you to fuck me, Zane." I feel the need to clarify. "With your cock."

He sucks in a breath and sputters. I can almost see him fighting off a cough on the other end of the phone. He wasn't expecting that answer. It would be funny if I wasn't so worried he'll say no.

"Em. You don't want..." He clears his throat again. "...you don't want me to take your virginity."

"I do." I launch into my explanation, my heart in my throat and wondering if I can convince him. "I told you it's not a religious thing and I'm not expecting champagne and rose petals and a big romantic gesture but if its going to be the sex I remember for the rest of my life, I want it to be a good memory."

"I can be memorable."

"I know you can."

He doesn't agree to do it but he doesn't say no, so I let it sit there between us. Suspended on the wireless threads out in the ether in the shape of a big fat question mark.

He breaks the silence like only Zane Wyatt can. Blunt and to the point.

"All this sex talk has made me horny."

I hum, letting my hand spread out across my belly. I let my fingers glide under my tank top, enjoying the warm glide of skin against skin. I let my hand drift lower and ease under the edge of my panties. I know where this is going: my first phone sex.

I gasp as my fingertip brushes my clit and I know Zane heard me because the next thing I hear across the line is him asking, "Em, are you wet? I'm so fucking hard, I hurt."

Chapter Ten

Zane

I can hear her arousal over the phone and I make no effort to hide my own.

I'm jacked up on the amazing show tonight, the relief that Eric is long gone and my own reaction to the conversation I just had with Emory. It's not like I haven't had a partner try to claim me before. No matter how it starts, in a bathroom stall at a club or on a real date, eventually the time comes when they want to be more than a fuck buddy. Or they want to be the only fuck buddy. I'm used to it.

I've just never had a time when that thought didn't make me want to run.

Emory pretty much laid out that she wants it be just the two of us and I never had one thought of ending the call. No, my first thought was that I don't want her to want anybody else. I don't want her to let anyone else touch her.

That is some crazy shit in my world. I don't think those kinds of thoughts have ever crossed my mind. So I'm more than willing to let a little phone sex distract me.

"I'm wet, Zane. My panties are soaked," Emory whispers into the phone and I undo the buttons on my jeans and shove my hand in there and drag out my erection.

I am hard, aching and hot to the touch as I start the stroke. Not slow and calculated to last. Nope. I start babbling, letting her see every dirty, pervy thought that is going through my mind right now.

"Em, all I can think about you letting me fuck your mouth. It was so perfect. *You* were so perfect."

Silence echoes across the line for so long that I think we've lost connection. And then I hear her voice, small and unusually timid for her.

"I don't know how to do this. It's so much easier with you right here with me. I'm nervous for some reason."

She just asked me to take her v-card and now she's embarrassed to dirty talk over the phone? I smile and slow my stroke down as I settle back against the cushions and think of how to make her feel like I'm right there.

"Don't be nervous. It's just us. Em and Zane." I lower my voice and let it go low and easy, making sure my drawl coats every word. "You just listen to me and I'll get you there, baby. Okay?"

"Okay."

"Are you touching yourself?"

"Yes." She ends the word on a gasp so I know she's telling the truth.

"Good. I wish I was there, fingers along your pussy lips. You get so wet and it smells so good. Salty. Real. With a hint of that citrus shampoo you use. Pure heaven." I restart the slow stroke on my cock, letting my arousal spin out as I tease hers from her secret places. "I love getting inside you, the way your body clings to me. So pretty. So tight. I need all your sweet, juicy girl lube so when I fuck you its smooth and deep. You'd lift your hips to me and beg me with your body to put my mouth on you. You want me to suck your clit, don't you baby?"

"Yes...oh." Her answer is more moan than words and a drop of slick pre-come rolls down my shaft in response.

"Baby, I'm so hard. My cock is leaking with how much I want to be inside you but I'll keep my fingers inside your heat. I'll touch you, stroke you to get you ready for me. Right now, I've got to have a taste of your hard, pink, pretty clit. Do you want that?"

"Yes."

"Beg me, Emory."

"Please, Zane," she whimpers across the line and I can

hear her moving against the sheets of her bunk. I wish I was there with her, if only to see the desire in her eyes and on her face.

"You need to better than that, Em. Beg like you really want it." I put an edge of mean in my voice and I hold my breath to see if it will turn her off or dial her up to a higher level of burn.

"Please Zane. Suck my clit. Suck it hard and make me come."

Oh yeah. I've got her now and she's got me. I'm on the edge but I need to wait for her go first. I need to hear her moan my name.

"You going to come on my face if I do it? Or are you going to tease me? Make me want it until I beg?"

"No, I'll come for you. Please."

"Then do it, baby. Come for me. Touch your clit and let me hear it. Now."

One. Two. Three. Four. Five. Six seconds pass and I hear her suck in a breath and that momentary pause and whimper she does in the back of her throat when she flies apart. And then she growls out my name with a ferocity that aims right for my balls.

I come hard, spilling over my hand and my jeans like a teenager. I grit my teeth and then choke out a laugh as I keep coming, over and over.

All I hear on her end is rapid breathing and hums of pleasure as I try to catch my breath and say something with the two brain cells I have left.

"Damn, Zane." Emory finally says on her end and I laugh.

"I know. I know."

"That was my first phone sex," she confesses and I bite back my laugh. I don't want her to think I'm making fun of her. She just makes me happy with all her earnest honesty right after being such a white-hot sex kitten.

"I like being your first." It's the truth and it makes me think about another first I'd like to be. "I'll do it, Em. I'll fuck you if you want me to."

Big pause and I wonder if she's changed her mind. I try not to think to hard about the disappointment that builds up in me at that thought.

"I want you to."

"I'd love to be your first." I pause not really sure how to proceed. I've never been asked to be someone's first lover before. I go with my gut. "I'll work it out. Make it nice for you, okay?"

"You don't have to do that, Zane."

"I want to. Don't worry about it."

"I think down deep you're a nice guy and a closet romantic, Zane Wyatt," she teases as a yawn travels over the line.

"Shut up and go to sleep. Don't tell anybody that you think I'm a nice guy. It will ruin my reputation."

"Yeah, yeah," she says right before she hangs up the phone. "Your secret is safe with me."

Chapter Eleven

Emory

"I can't believe that we just spent the last two days recording our songs."

Zane looks up at me and gives me a wild, happy grin as he leans over the shoulder of Leon, the sound engineer and talks about stuff that really doesn't make sense to me. All I know is that when they turn the sound back on and our song rolls like thunder out of the speakers, I can't breathe.

I have to thank Kit for this opportunity. Fans at her show videotaped our performance of *Lies and Love* and the footage went viral. Every media outlet you can think of started calling us and Kit sent us here to record a digital single to put up on iTunes and milk the notoriety for all its worth. Good for the tour and good us. Everybody wins.

But I still can't believe that I'm here. Six months has been an amazing game change for me and I feel the need to pinch myself every second of the day. I'm just glad I have Kit and Zane to walk with me. I'd be lost without them.

"That's not me," I say, backing up as if to emphasize my point. "There is no way I sound like that."

Leon, the sound guy shakes his head and adjusts a slide on the board. "It's all you. I don't need to mix with of your voices. Pure gold in the pipes. You guys are lucky."

I look at Zane and just stare, unable to believe the whirlwind that has become my life. He straightens up and walks over to me, his hands cupping my face as he leans down to whisper a soft kiss against my lips and quick swipe of his nose along my cheek. He nuzzles into my hair and says into my ear, "Emory Cabell, your voice makes me hard and I want to cry every time I hear it. That is *all* you and don't you doubt it."

"You're crazy," I whisper back.

"Only about you," he says before pulling away, weaving our fingers together and leading me over to our guitars. I blink and think about what he just said and wonder if he even realizes it. Zane is an affectionate man, always touching and always making sure you know that you are the center of his attention. It's quite overwhelming and I have to work overtime to not read too much into it. This is just the honeymoon phase of any relationship, no matter how temporary.

He picks up his guitar and sits down on the sofa and I ease my but down on the coffee table in front of him. Our knees bump and I adjust my position so that one of my knees is between his and I scoot in closer. "Okay, listen to this and tell me if you think it needs to be change on the bridge."

He plays the notes, switching it up when it gets to point where the bridge flows into the resolution chorus. It sounds good but I'm not sure.

"Play it again," I ask and he does as I ask, making a slight adjustment that I like. It's darker and keeps the driving beat. I nod as he continues, urging him to go with that version. "I like it."

He smiles up at me and heads into the final chorus and starts to sing. I join in and we switch up the arrangement, shifting the harmonies and goofing around with the lyrics until we are both laughing. Leon snorts out a belly laugh over the system and we lose it again. I wipe tears away from my eyes and inhale deeply to catch my breath.

"I've never had so much fun in my life," I say and I mean it.

"The music is a good time, yeah?"

"And the company," I answer and feel the blush creep across my collarbone. What a cheesball thing to say.

Zane leans over and gives me a swift hard kiss followed

by a gentle rub of our noses together and then goes back to playing. It's new, a song that I don't know and I watch him as he works through the chords and the strum. It's sensual and slow and I start working on lyrics in my head. Ones that deal with the dark, mouths open, and bodies moving in a rhythm calculated to make it good.

It's hot and he's so sexy with his dark hair escaping the leather thong tying it off his face. I stare, taking advantage of his focus to ogle and memorize. The dark scruff of his goatee, the long fingers with callouses that feel so good against my skin, and his lush, full lips. Yummy goodness from the top of his head to the bottom of his very sexy, large feet.

Zane looks up and catches me in mid-drool.

"You can't look at me like that on stage," he says, leaning in close, our mouths almost touching.

"Why not?"

"Because this right here. . ." He plays the chords, making them rise at a slow, languid pace. "This is how you sound when you come. That little catch in the back of your throat right before you lose it."

"What? You're serious?" I lean in closer to catch his every word. I am mermerized by him. And not just a little.

"Completely." He nods as he continues to play, smiling at me with his fallen angel smile that always convinces me to follow him into the dark. "Em, if you look at me like that when I play it everyone will know it's my favorite fucking sound in the world and that I spend all my time wondering when I can hear it again."

"Oh hell, how do you do that?" I lean in and brush a kiss across his mouth, sneaking a small taste with my tongue. "How do you say shit like that to me and make me so crazy?"

"I just speak the truth." Zane's eyes are dark and sultry and I don't know how I'm ever going to perform this song without having a spontaneous orgasm on the spot.

"Be careful. Your closet romantic is showing."

He grins at me and keeps playing.

"Isn't this just the cutest scene ever?" A woman's voice

cuts into our little world and I look over my shoulder to see who it is.

A woman I do not know at all. Tall, auburn haired and wearing an outfit that can only be described as a "power suit". I look down at my jean capris and tank top and wonder which one of us didn't get the wardrobe memorandum.

"Zane, are you going to introduce me to your friend?" She walks towards us and throws her expensive looking purse on the table next to me. We both stand and I prepare to put out my hand to shake hers and she totally bypasses me for Zane.

She has perfect aim and hits the bulls-eye when she lands a kiss right on his mouth.

His mouth. The one that I want to claim.

I clench my hands into fists to resist the urge to smack her. He's not mine. Not even a little bit and he's never said he was.

He pulls back and looks at me, his expression mostly unreadable except for the embarrassment I see making the tips of his ears turn red. Zane rallies like the professional performer he is and begins the introductions, nice and smooth. No fuss.

"Maureen Richards. She's one of the A&R directors at Waterworld Media." He turns to me, tucking my hand into his and pulling me close. "This is Emory Cabell. Talented songwriter and singer and someone you'll be hearing more about."

I stick my hand out to her and smile. "It's nice to meet you."

"Now, *that's* an accent." She gives my hand a barely-there shake and returns all of her attention to Zane. "You like them fresh off the farm now?"

I want to kill her.

***

Zane

Oh sweet baby Jesus.

Maureen is spoiling for a fight and Emory will give her

one if I don't intervene. It's not that I don't think Em can hold her own but I'm not going to put her in the crossfire of a battle where I am the intended target. She would only be collateral damage.

"Okay Maureen, what are you doing here?"

Emory and Maureen are squared off like two prizefighters in the ring, ignoring me so I step in between them, forcing the end of the stare off with my body.

"Maureen, we're kind of busy here so why don't you tell me why you're here?"

She blinks up at me and smiles. It isn't really friendly, in fact I would call it feral and at one time I would have called it sexy. Not so much anymore.

"I need to talk to you about your career."

"I'm going to grab a coffee," Emory says and cuts me a glance as she walks away. Her back is rigid and she's pissed. When I look at Maureen I let all of my irritation show.

"Why can't you be nice?" I ask, knowing that it's a stupid question. Maureen isn't nice because she doesn't want to be. "You know what? Forget it. I know better than to expect the impossible."

"Did you check her ID, Zane? Did she actually graduate high school?"

"She's nineteen and that is not why you're here," I prod her on, hoping she gets to the point. "Emory and I have plans so..."

"Right. She's probably got a curfew."

"Maureen," I say, making sure she hears the warning. "Leave Emory alone."

"Fine. I don't have time for toddlers anyway. I need you to get me an answer on the offer we made you."

"I told you that I'm not taking it." I cross my arms over chest and shake my head for emphasis. We've been around this block about a million times. "I'm not giving up creative control."

She smiles at me and this time she pours it all on and it is full of dirty promises. She reaches out and runs a fingernail over my forearm. There was a time when she got me hard and kept me that way. We never did get together no matter how hard she tried. We were always a failure to launch.

"You'll be working with me. I'll let you do whatever you want," she cajoles, her voice low and laced with sugar. Too sweet. Too syrupy. It has never sounded genuine to me and now is no different.

"Not good enough. You wouldn't agree to that and I don't know why you expect me to. Send me a better offer through my agent and we can talk."

She considers me, her teeth biting into her lower lip in either contemplation or seduction. I'm not entirely sure. I don't really care. I twist around to see if I can find Emory.

"Am I boring you, Zane?" Maureen's voice is laced with ice and the already chilly studio plummets into the arctic zone. I swallow, knowing I need to tread carefully. Nashville is a small town and Waterworld is a big label. I cannot afford to burn any bridge at this stage in my career.

I turn to her and smile, turning on a little bit of my charm. "No, but we only have this studio for a little while longer and we have more stuff to do before we can call it a night."

Emory comes back into the studio, a cup of coffee in her hand a frown on her face. She barely glances in our direction, concentrating on whatever Leon is telling her. I don't like the distance I feel between us. My fingers itch to touch the golden fall of hair that shields her expression from me, to sweep it back and let the silk of it caress my skin.

"Oh, you *like* this one." Maureen says from beside me and I look over to see her pick her purse up off the table. "I thought you were smart enough not to shit where you eat, Zane. At least that's what you told me when you turned me down."

I wince at the tone of hurt in her words but I can't deny the truth of them. I open my mouth to answer but I've got nothing. I'm not taking her offer and I'm not sleeping with her. We don't have much to talk about.

She laughs and the sound is bitter and sharp. "Don't freak out Zane. When you tired of playing Romper Room and you want to get serious about getting a record out, call me."

"Goodbye Maureen."

She takes another long look at me and then turns towards the door, her hand waving goodbye over her shoulder. "Take my offer."

I watch her leave and give a deep exhale.

"Is she pissed of that you won't be sleeping with her tonight?" Emory asks behind me.

I turn to see if *she's* pissed and I'm met with stormy green eyes and fierce emotion. Emory is a passionate person and I can see that it extends to all of her emotions and not just the ones in bed.

"I never slept with Maureen," I answer and decide that full disclosure is probably the best plan right now. "I thought about it. She wanted it."

"So, what stopped you?"

"I always figured that sleeping with Maureen would be a full contact sport, a cage match. I never want to work that hard in bed."

Her lips twitch with the hint of a smile and she dips her head to hide it from me. I could end it here but I figure she needs to know all of it.

"Her label offered me a deal but it wasn't what I wanted so I turned it down."

"And she doesn't want to take no for an answer?"

"Nope." I move close enough to pull Emory into my arms and get this day back on track and away from anymore talk about Maureen. "I don't want to talk about her. I want to talk about the surprise I have planned for you."

She curls her fingers in my t-shirt and yanks me close. "For me? What is it?"

"Yeah, no. I'm not going to tell you. That would spoil the fun."

"Will I like it?"

I lean down and kiss her, unable to resist the allure of

Emory. Her arms twine around my neck and she curls into me, her lips open and her body soft. I could stay here and do this all night but I really want to show her the surprise.

"I hope you love it."

Chapter Twelve

Zane

"What did you do?" Emory asks, her eyes wide as I tug her into the suite at the Hermitage Hotel.

Everything I arranged is here: the champagne, the rose petals on the king-size bed.

Suddenly I'm really worried that this was the wrong thing to do. Too presumptuous. Too manipulative. I can't tell from her tone if this was a good move or a bad move. When she turns to look at me I scramble for another reason but my mind is a total blank. I go for the truth of it.

"Your first time should be special and I think you deserve more than my mattress sitting on a box spring on the floor."

She stares at me for so long that I really start to worry. It's clear that I might have completely misinterpreted what was going on here.

"If I got it wrong, we don't have to anything more than what we've been doing. We can just fool around, order some room service and pay-per-view. We can enjoy a big bed that isn't on wheels for a change."

Emory drops her bag on the floor and walks over to me, her lips curving up in a sexy half-smile. She stops in front of me and lean up and kisses me. Not hot, not wet. It's almost chaste but the power of it rocks me on feet. I reach out and catch her face gently between my hands as she pulls away.

"This is perfect," she whispers. "Thank you."

I pull her close again and run my nose along the soft skin of her cheek. She closes her eyes and nuzzles back, a deep sigh escaping her lips and settling over me. Calming me. Suddenly, this feels right.

"Zane?" She asks, soft and sweet.

"Yeah?"

"Make love to me."

I look down at her and smile, watching as she slowly grins back. "I'd love to."

We lean towards each other again and I dive in for another kiss, licking at her lips until she parts them. Her hands settle on my shoulders, her fingers digging into the muscle there before sliding down my chest until they reach the hem. She tugs on the material at the same time I walk backwards and ease us both down on the bed. With a laugh I give in to her and help her lift the shirt over my head and toss it to the floor.

Emory dips her head and kisses the tattoo on my bicep, and then the one across my pectoral. She nips the flesh just below my collarbone and laughs when I jump.

"I love your ink. So sexy."

"You have too many clothes on," I say, easing my fingers under the hem of her top and quickly getting it off and out of the way. Her bra is a light pink and almost blends in with the pale blush of her skin. "Goddam, you're beautiful."

Emory slides her hands into my hair and tugs me to her and takes my mouth in a kiss full of longing and hot desire. I give in and lean us both back onto the coverlet, wrapping my arms around her and covering her with my body. She arches up into me, my jeans and her skirt an unwanted barrier between us.

"I've got to get these off you, baby. It's been too long since I got to touch you." I lean up on one elbow and brace myself, my other fingers unbuttoning and easing the zipper down on her skirt. I push it down to her thighs and she wriggles it off the rest of the way. I run my fingers down her arm, across her hip, the lightest touch between her legs. "You're so hot here already. Are you wet?"

"I'm always wet for you Zane. It's becoming a problem."

"Not for me it isn't." I laugh and grab her hand, kissing her finger, then her palm, and finally her wrist where her pulse is fluttering under the skin. "I want to see all of you, Em."

She nods and sits up, allowing me to unclasp her bra and slide it down and off her body. Her breasts are heavy, the nipples tight and my mouth waters to taste them but I postpone that in favor of getting her completely naked. I slide down beside her and reach up and slide her panties off. Emory lying back against the pristine white sheets with the rose petals sprinkled there is enough to steal my breath.

She's long and lean, her skin flawless and soft. The rose pink of her nipples and the deeper pink of her pussy entice me to taste and lick. I wedge my body in between her legs and crawl up her body until we are face-to-face. I look down at her and a wave of possessiveness grabs me and I take her mouth in a kiss.

This one is nothing like the others. It is deep, and fierce and sends sparks of fire under my skin. My cock is hard and heavy against my hip and I slowly grind it against the softer span of her belly. Her hands wedge between us and she distracts me from her mouth when she unzips me and starts shoving the denim over my hips and down my thighs. We keep kissing, laughing lightly when we both have to work at kicking the jeans entirely off.

When my erection settles against the slick heat of her sex, all laughter is lost in a bone deep groan from us both.

I reach down and grab her thigh, lifting until I can slide the entire length of my dick up and down, in between her wet folds. I kiss her lazily, taking my time and allowing us both the chance to taste and feel before we lose all control. We rock against each other, letting the pleasure build.

"You feel so good," Emory sighs breathlessly against my mouth.

"This is nothing compared to how good I'm going to make you feel."

I move down her body until I can suck on her nipples. I lick them both, alternating between the two, admiring the way they darken and glisten with my spit. I suck the right one into my mouth, covering the left with my hand when she arches up on a cry of pleasure. Her legs spread even wider and my cock is slippery with her arousal as she bucks up against me. Emory's fingers dig into my scalp as she tries to keep me in place and guides my mouth the skin I have neglected.

"Please Zane." She writhes underneath me, her body begging for something I'm not ready to give her yet. "Do it."

"Be patient, Emory. I'm not rushing this for you."

"I don't need all this foreplay," she complains but there's no heat in it.

"Too bad. I love foreplay and I want to lick you all over. Your nipples are sweet and I know you're pussy will be even sweeter." I run a finger along her lips, and spread the slick lube already there. "I'll eat you until your thighs are slippery and wet with it and then I'll slide into you with my cock and make you come all over again."

She curses at me under breath and I smile, relieved that she wants it as bad as I do.

I press a final kiss against her nipple and lift over my head to grab her hands and place them on her breasts. She lifts her head and looks at me, a question in her eyes.

"So, be a good girl and touch yourself while I make you come. I want you good and wet when I fuck you."

Chapter Thirteen

Emory

I'll do anything he wants when he talks to me like that.

Eric never did. He was always careful, even when he was really horny but I never wanted to be on that pedestal. You can't let go when you're up that high.

Zane is making me crazy with the slow burn tonight. I'm on fire, crazy to have him inside me and he's taking his time.

"I want you inside me," I beg and I feel him shiver. Good, I don't want to be the only one on the edge.

He eases down my body and bows his head to press a kiss against my hip, then at the top of my curls, the inside of my thigh. I angle my head so that I can watch him and our eyes lock when he dips down with purpose. He stops and reaches up to lazily stroke my nipple.

"I thought I told you to touch yourself," he says and then licks once and only once across my clit. "Do it if you want more."

I don't have to be told twice when I need his mouth on me. I cup both my breasts in my hand and begin a slow, teasing swipe of my nipples with my thumbs. He gives me dark look and lowers his face to my sex.

His mouth is hot and wet as he kisses my pussy, sucking on me, licking. He uses his fingers to caress me, to tease me with shallow dips inside my body. I try to grind down on it, to force him deeper but he refuses, keeping me on the edge with it.

I ache with my need. My skin is hot and slick with sweat as I strain to come.

"Lift up baby, " he says and I follow his lead as he slips a pillow under my hips and raises me higher off the bed.

Zane settles back between my legs, his mouth tracing down my sex with light teasing kisses and then lower. I gasp in surprise and my legs spread even wider when his shoulders nudge them apart. I'm wide open to him, and anything he wants to do to me and I shiver in anticipation.

His thumb glides over my clit, spreading my lube and making me moan as I feel the orgasm building inside me. Zane laps at me as if he's starving for something he can only get by making me feel good. When he begins to fuck me with his tongue, I grab the coverlet and twist it between my fingers as the first wave hits me.

"Zane. Oh god." I hump against him as the hot, tingly glow of pleasure rips through me. It's amazing and awful in its intensity and I try to pull away from it, to distance myself from it but he doesn't let me. His hands grip my hips and he drags slow, lazy, wet, hot kisses along the tender skin of thighs, over my hip and across my belly until I'm relaxed and limp.

He reaches down to where his jeans are bunched at the bottom of the bed and produces a condom. I watch as he kneels between my legs and smooths the rubber down his length. He smiles, that's devil's own grin that makes me clench my thighs in anticipation as he strokes himself from tip to root.

Zane leans over and kisses me, his tongue stroking along my lower lip and I feel the head of his cock pressing against the entrance to my body and inside me. I gasp at the stretch, my hand reaching to grasp his hip and urge him on.

He drops his forehead against mine and groans, flexing his hips to push deeper. I can feel the strain of his muscles as he struggles to control himself as he slowly fills me up. He lifts his head and kisses me hungrily, sliding his fingers into my hair as he slowly rocks his hips against mine. Our tongues slide together as he continues the slow thrusts. All the way out and then back in. I can feel every inch of him.

I lift my leg higher and he slides in deeper and the fullness and pleasure interrupts the kiss. I slide my palms over the planes of his back, the bulge of his biceps until I can wrap them around his neck and keep him there with me. We are nothing but a slow glide, sloppy kisses, and gasping, aching breaths.

"Please baby, harder. I need you." The words out of my mouth before I even realize I've said them and it flips a switch in Zane.

He freezes for a moment and then the tension inside him snaps and he picks up the pace and pulls my leg up higher so that he can plunge in deep. His cock touches all of me on the inside while the hard plane of his pelvic bone rubs against my clit with every thrust. He kisses me, swallowing my louder moans and sighs as I release my hold around his neck and grip the bunched sheets under us.

"Oh Christ," Zane whispers against my throat and it feels like a prayer. His voice is broken and needy when he pleads. "Tell me that it's good. Tell me."

"So good. So fucking good," I answer in between the deep lungfuls of air I try to inhale as a new, sharper tension coils in my belly. I've come before but this is different, the fullness making the pleasure almost unbearable. My skin is tight and hot and I don't know how it will keep me inside. I feel like I'm going to come apart. "Zane."

He must hear the fear and joy in my voice be cause he pulls back and all I can see is the copper rimmed onyx of his eyes focused on my He murmurs my name softly and then kisses me roughly, a quick thrust of tongue before he breaks it.

"Baby, just let go. I'm here with you. Right here. Let go and take me with you." His words are tinted with dark need and a gentle affection that makes my chest ache and my pussy clench around his cock. "Come on. All over me."

A drop of his sweat rolls down his nose and hits my breast, his movements sharper and focused as I lift my own hips to meet him each and every time.

"Yeah, fuck me. Em...take me. Take all of me," he growls and I close my eyes as the pleasure slams into me with his deep, hard thrust.

I claw at his back, my nails digging in like I'm afraid that he'll stop, that he leave me here alone in this intoxicating blend of sex and friendship and illusion.

Zane yells and bucks his hips, digging in his knees to get more leverage as he shoves his cock into me faster and in time with the beat of his orgasm. He slumps against me, his large, hard body covering mine as a final act of compassion from this man who is such a strange mix of elusive Peter Pan, loyal friend, and tender lover. His fingers shake as they cup my face and gently pull me to him for a soft kiss.

We lie there for a while, long past the time when his softening cock has left my body empty and aching. I have him wrapped in my arms, holding his full weight against me as his fingertips trace a hypnotic pattern on my shoulder.

"We need a shower," he whispers against my temple.

"I..." I bite my lip and wonder if I should say what immediately came to mind. He senses my hesitation and huffs out a barely-there laugh.

"I've had my mouth on your pussy and you've had my cock in your mouth and inside you, just tell me. Embarrassment between us is pointless."

It's blunt and so totally Zane and it is completely, 100% right.

"I don't want to shower because I want your scent on me when I wake up tomorrow. I want to smell like us."

He groans and lifts up on one elbow to look down at me, the smirk on his face sexy and confident. "That is the hottest thing anyone has ever said to me."

"Yeah?"

"Yeah." He kisses me, gently as if he's sipping from my mouth. "You were so fucking good, Little Bird. I want to do it again. Please tell me it was so good you want to do it again."

"I want to do it again."

"Thank fuck," he murmurs and then kisses me deeply, his tongue exploring me slowly and thoroughly. When we pull apart we are both breathing hard and he swallows hard before speaking. "Thank you, Emory. Thank you for letting it be me."

"I'm glad it was you, Zane."

He pauses and I can see hesitation as it clouds his eyes and roots itself in the little furrow between his eyebrows. In spite of what he just said, a brief spark of panic lights up in my gut. I have no idea what he is thinking and right now I don't want the spell broken. I just want to hide here in this beautiful suite with the sexiest man I've ever met and pretend that this is my life. The one I came here to find.

"I've been thinking about what you said on the phone the other night."

I still have no idea what he is talking about so I just wait, my heart pounding.

"I think I want you to have a claim on me," he says and dips his head so I can't look him in the eye. He's hiding from me, from this and I'm going to let him because it scares the shit out me too. "I don't know what you call it but I want you to expect to be the one in my bed."

"Like a boyfriend?" I ask, stunned by where this conversation is gone.

He meets my eyes again and I see the struggle going on in his head. New territory for him but he's being honest with me, and right now, that's enough.

"You know what? We don't need a label. Not us." I say and push a curl of his dark hair from his face and smile. "Let's just write music and have more sex and see where this goes."

The relief on his face is clear and I tamp the tiny flare of disappointment in my gut because he's not ready to make some commitment that I'm not sure I'm ready for either. I like where this is going though.

A lot more than I'm ready to admit.

I'm glad when he lets it go with a sheepish smile and the second best suggestion I've heard all night.

"Are you hungry? This place makes the best grilled cheese you've ever tasted."

Chapter Fourteen

Zane

"This is the best twenty-one dollar grilled cheese I have ever had," Emory says.

She sits on the other end of the window seat in the hotel room, wrapped in the complementary robe with one hand holding the sandwich and the other holding a french fry slathered in ketchup. Her hair is a mess and she has no makeup on but I think she looks gorgeous.

"What? You don't agree?" She asks, biting down on the french fry with a playful chomp. She watches me, pausing when I just keep staring at her. "Do I have ketchup in my hair or something?"

I laugh. "No. You just look really good."

"Better than this twenty-one dollar grilled cheese?"

"Way better." I lean over the distance between us and press a kiss to her mouth. It is short and salty and I while I take every opportunity to delve in and taste her, I pull back and smile down at her when it is done. "You okay?"

"Are you asking if I'm feeling any side effects from letting you take my v-card?"

"Smartass." I deliver another swift kiss to her lips and lift my hand to glide my fingers along her cheek. She closes her eyes and leans into my touch. "I'm asking if it was good for you. Was it what you wanted?"

Two heartbeats pass and she opens her eyes, the green vivid and bright and something else that causes my breath to catch in my throat. Damn her, How does she do that?

"If it was the time I'm going to remember for the rest of

my life, I'm glad it was you. You make good memories, Zane."

I blush and the heat of the sensation is foreign to me. It's insane the amount of pride and possession I feel right now knowing that we have shared this and no one else will ever have it with Emory. I let the sensation linger for a few more seconds before I push it away.

"I think it took two of us to make it something worth remembering," I say, dipping to press a quick kiss to the tip of her nose. It's her turn to blush when I pull back to look at her. I smile and get up, maneuvering us until I I'm sitting in her spot and she's leaning against me, the warm expanse of her body against me. The slow exhale we both make testifies to the fact that we are both where we want to be. We look out of the window and soak in the lights of the old capital building. "Tell me. First song you ever sang in public."

She thinks for a bit and then smiles. "*Jolene*. I launched into it at the Sunday School picnic and I thought my mama and all the ladies of the missionary society were going to die when I got to the verse where I'm crying because he calls her name in his sleep."

"Oh hell. How old were you?"

"Seven? Eight?" Emory giggles at the memory and I shift behind her as the movement vibrates against my semi-hard cock. It would only take a little bit for me to go for round two but I'm following her lead. I want to fall on her like a ravenous beast but this is her night. I want it to be what she wants. What she needs. "She told my daddy off all the way home but he just winked at me and showed me how to work the chord progression even smoother."

"I think I would have liked your dad," I say and nuzzle against the silk of her hair. I inhale deeply. She smells like citrus and sunshine and sex. I loop my arms around her waist, dipping my fingers inside the flap of her robe until I find the warm satin of the skin on her belly. She hums and rests her head in the crook of my shoulder, rubbing her cheek against me in a gentle sweep of affection.

"He was pretty great. I'm just sorry that he had to lie to

be happy."

"You and Kit are okay with how that all went down?"

"We can't change it and it really wasn't up to us," she says, her voice soft. "She's got some anger for being left alone with her grandparents and her mom but she understands why he did it. I know for me I've decided that I need to just leave it in the past and embrace the fact that I have a sister now. To do anything else will make me nuts."

The silence stretches out between us again. Comfortable while also charged with the electricity that spans between us all the time. I've gotten used to feeling like I'm holding a live wire whenever she's around. It still feels dangerous but I'm starting to crave the edge of never knowing whether the spark is going to give me a thrill or kill me.

"Where did you grow up Zane?" Emory breaks into my thoughts and brings me to a topic I've had on my mind the last week.

"You'll see it tomorrow when we play at the PNC Arena in Raleigh. I grew up in a small town called Ivy, just outside of town."

She shifts to look at up at me, her eyes wide. "Really? How do you feel about going home? Happy? Nervous?"

"I guess I need to figure it out since my family is coming to the show," I offer with a tight smile and a shrug I know isn't convincing. "Mom, Dad, my brothers and their wives. The whole gang."

"Is this the first show of yours they'll see?"

"Yeah." I consider telling her the entire truth of it and decide to go for it when I look into her eyes and remember what a gift she gave me tonight. Our friendship is obviously the kind that can withstand a little bit of truth. "I finally feel like I've gotten to place where I can hold my head up to my old man. One of the opening acts for Kit's tour is proof that this music thing wasn't a waste of my time."

The words are still as bitter on my tongue as they were to hear them all those years ago.

"So this is a way to throw it in their faces?"

I shake my head and let it all out. The real truth.

"My dad wasn't the only one to draw a line in the sand all those years ago. I screwed up and so did he. It's time to try to leave it in the past like you and Kit have done." I take a deep breath but I fail to keep the emotion out of my voice. "I don't know how it's going to be but I miss my family and if there is a way to fix this mess, I need to take it. This is the first step, I think."

Emory shifts around even more to face me, her fingers trace along my lips and I press a kiss to them and do it again when she smiles.

"It will work out, Zane."

Oh hell. There's that simple honesty from her again. More seductive than any low-cut dress or come-on line. It's what makes her so unique, so real. Its what makes me want to stake my claim, to enter into that zone where promises are made. When I said it earlier, the words just tumbled out and once they were spoken I wasn't sure if I could back them up. I want her. I really like being with her but I'm not sure I'm ready yet and somehow she knew it and gave me the space to figure it out.

"Are you a fortune teller Little Bird?" I smile and lean down for a soft kiss. I linger, coaxing her into a series of progressively deeper kisses that leave us both panting for air. I tug aside the lapel of robe until I can stroke her skin, the taut pebble of her nipples, the tender underside of her breast and lower. She spreads her legs for my touch and I groan when I discover how wet she is. "Jesus, Em. I want to be inside you again. Please."

"I need to check my crystal ball," she teases, gasping when I enter her with one finger and stroke her clit with my thumb. I smile against her mouth when she moans.

"So, what does it say? Am I in or not?"

"Not yet..." She pulls back and flashes me that dark angel grin that is quickly becoming my very favorite thing about her. "...but you will be."

And that's all the future I need to know right now.

Chapter Fifteen

Zane

The farm looks exactly the same.

I pull the rental car into the gravel area just to the right of the house under the crepe myrtles. They are in full bloom, the tiny white flowers sometimes raining down with the breeze and giving the illusion of summer snow.

"This is lovely, Zane," Emory says from the passenger seat, her big green eyes taking it all in. "What kind of farm is it?"

We unfasten our seatbelts and slide out of the car. I open the trunk and grab our overnight bags, hefting them over my shoulder. Voices drift up from the back of the house, kids squealing and the low rumble of adult conversation. I hold out my hand to her, relieved when she weaves her fingers with mine. Once again, I'm glad I asked her to come with me. Emory's gentle strength calms me and the cowardly part of me knows she'll be a great buffer between me and my dad.

"Cattle. Soybeans. Corn." I look around the land, noting the new barn behind the one I used to clean out when I was a kid. "I'm sure my brother David has changed some things. He runs the farm now and has an agricultural degree."

I follow the path around the house and duck under the lattice arbor covered in mom's roses and emerge into the bright sunshine of the back yard. Everybody is here and they all turn to look at me at the same time. It would be funny if I didn't have a million butterflies in my stomach. Emory squeezes my hand lightly and I look down at her and smile.

"I'm glad you came," I say.

"I'm glad you asked me." She smiles and nods towards

my waiting family. "Introduce me Wyatt."

I laugh and tug her with me as I face the gauntlet of hugs and kisses from my brothers, their wives and kids. We are swarmed by the little ones, anxious to get a close look at the visitor.

"Emory, I would call out the names of all these brats but my brothers keep producing children faster than I can get the names memorized," I joke as she is engulfed in hugs from all the little Wyatts. They practically tackle her to the ground with their enthusiasm but I can see that she loves it.

"If I could just figure out how these babies are made I might be able to make it stop." David jokes as he picks up his youngest daughter, Ava. She reaches her chunky hand out to Emory, her face covered in what looks like watermelon.

"Well, what I heard is that when a mommy and a daddy love each other very much and share the same toothpaste, babies happen," I answer, keeping my voice deadpan and completely serious.

My seven year-old nephew, Stevie disagrees. "Uncle Zane, that's wrong. Babies are made when grown-ups kiss and the male puts his penis—"

David uses his free hand to cover up his son's mouth before he can spill the secrets of the universe.

"Stevie, I told you we weren't going to talk about that in front of the little kids," David warns and flashes an embarrassed smile at Emory. "He rides on the school bus with older kids who tell him *everything*."

"Do they get it right? Or are they passing on bad info?" Emory asks.

"It is scary how much they get right. I blame it on the internet." He lets go of Stevie and extends his hand to her. "I'm David. You were amazing last night. Best show I've ever seen."

"Thank you so much." She blushes and immediately tries to change the subject like she always does when it involves her talent. "I'm excited to meet all of you."

"I'll introduce you to the rest of the clan," I say and grab her hand again, leading her over to the brick patio covered in lounge chairs and tables. We spend a lot of time out here in the summer and my mom makes sure it's comfortable. I point to each person as I go around the crowd. "This is David's wife Susan. My other brother Sean and his wife Cathy."

She shakes hands and smiles at them all and I can see that they are already smitten. Emory has that gift on and off the stage, one look and most people are hooked. I know she intrigued me on first sight.

"This is my mom," I say and release Emory long enough to wrap my mother in a big hug. She squeezes me tight and I grunt under the pressure. "Mom, let go! I can't breathe."

"If you came home more often I wouldn't have to squeeze you so hard," She teases while she releases me only to give me a visual inspection from head to toe. "You need to eat."

"I eat fine. Ask Emory."

"If you count pizza as the only major food group, he eats all the time," Emory says and throws me under the bus with a look that says she's not sorry. My mom chuckles and pulls my guest into a fierce embrace that makes her squeak in surprise. I flash her a you-deserve-that look and lean against the picnic table. "Thank you for having me, Mrs. Wyatt."

"Call me Sylvia," my mom says as she lets her go. "You were really wonderful last night Emory. You have so much talent."

"So does Zane. Does he get it from your or Mr. Wyatt?" Emory asks, looking around my mom to my dad. He's standing by the grill and turning the burgers and when he looks up, his face has its usual stoic expression. Emory's smile dims and I know what she sees.

James Wyatt. Man of steel and granite. Every inch of him covered in sharp edges and thorns.

My father is not unkind man but he is not easy. He grew up poor, working a farm with his father and grandfather and sometimes taking on other jobs to pay the bills. He is solid and reliable and honest to a fault but he is not soft or welcoming. He is polite but never expressive.

If we were any more different, I'd be on Mars.

"He doesn't get it from me, I can assure you of that," he says and motions for Sean to come over and take his place by dinner. He wipes his hand on a towel tucked into his back pocket and extends it to Emory. "I'm James Wyatt. We are pleased to have you here with us."

"The pleasure is mine," she answers, her tone subdued but still warm. I don't think he scares her but she's treading carefully. "Thank you for having me."

I walk over and extend my own hand to him. We don't hug but the grip is firm and it lingers for a few moments.

"It's good to see you dad."

"You too Zane."

"Burgers are ready," Sean says and I could kiss him for the perfect timing.

The flurry of movement to get all the food on the table, the kids settled at their table and our plates filled sucks all the tension out of the situation. We tuck into the food and talk about the farm and the neighbors. A typical dinner conversation for the Wyatt family.

"You doing okay?" I lean over and murmur against Emory's ear, letting my cheek rub against the silk of her hair.

"I'm good."

"Still glad you came?" Her only answer is a smile and her hand landing on my knee under the table.

"The show last night was amazing," David says. "You two are really great together. And that song? You blew me away!"

"I'm just sorry that you couldn't have stayed and met all of the band," Emory says.

"We had to get back. Farm work starts early," my father answers from his seat at the other end of the table. "We aren't usually up that late and it took us an hour to get home."

"Zane, did I tell you we got a call from the Charlotte Observer?" My mom's eyes are full of excitement and mischief and I groan with all the possibilities. "They wanted to talk to us about your childhood and such. I even gave them some of your pictures."

"Oh my God. Which ones?"

"The one of you in your Little League uniform and the one with the purple hair."

I groan and drop my fork on my plate so that I can cover my face. "You have a million pictures of me and you give him *that* one?"

"Purple hair?" Emory asks, her voice confused. I try to intervene but my brother David is happy to clear it up for her.

"Zane went through a period of time where he thought he was David Bowie or something."

"Iggy Pop," I mumble, the heat of my embarrassment crawling over my skin. "I went through a punk phase."

"Every time I would buy a tub of Kool-Aid, he'd use half of it to dye his hair," my mom says, her evil grin saying that she is happy to share all of my deep dark secrets with the world. "I finally had to hide it from him."

Emory starts laughing beside me, her belly laughs spurring all the others to join her and soon I'm surrounded by their snorts and useless attempts to get themselves under control. She looks at me, her eyelashes wet with her tears and I reach up to smooth them away with my thumb.

"You think that's funny?"

She inhales deeply, trying to stop the giggles. "I really do."

"So glad I could amuse you." I smile even though I don't think any of its funny. She's so pretty with her pink cheeks that I have to lean over and kiss her. I plan on it being short and sweet but she leans into my touch on her cheek and it lingers. Not porno or unsuitable for the kids sitting behind us but it is deep and filled with the longing for her that is always just under my skin.

We break apart and I realize that the laughing has stopped and everyone is eyeing us with curiosity. My sister-in-law, Cathy, looks ready to pounce with what I'm sure will be endless questions such as "How long have you been together?" and "Is it serious?" Topics I do not want to get into when I don't know the answer.

My mom saves me and I take back all the horrible things I was just thinking about her.

"The reporter wanted to know what we thought about your career. You know, as your parents."

My heart skips in my chest, a lead weight of crappy possibilities settles in my gut.

"And what did you say?"

"I didn't. Your father did."

My head swivels to the head of the table where my dad sits, quietly eating his potato salad and my stomach grabs that lead weight and does a dive into my toes. I can only imagine what he said and although I don't really want to know, I might have to do some damage control when the article hit the newsstands.

"What did you say dad?"

The table is silent because everyone wants to know. He's been so vocal about his opposition to my choice that I bet I can recite it without him saying a word.

"I told him that it takes a lot of guts to leave home against the advice of your parents and go to a city where you know no one and chase a dream that most people never achieve. I told him that as a father I couldn't be more proud."

My dad looks up and meets my eyes and what I see there is something I never thought I would see: respect. Not approval. Not understanding. But, I'll take it. It's more than I could have asked for.

I stare for several long moments before I finally find my voice. It takes a couple of short coughs but I eventually croak it out.

"Thanks dad."

"You're welcome."

He turns to Sean and asks about some fertilizer and gradually the conversation turns to topics that do not require me to contribute. Thank fuck, because I couldn't talk now if my life depended on it.

Emory's hand finds mine under the table and she leans over to whisper in my ear," That's good."

I hold on to her warmth and blink away the emotion pooling in my eyes, pulling myself together enough to nod and whisper back to her.

"The best."

Chapter Sixteen

Emory

I can't sleep.

I'm lying in Zane's childhood bed and staring up at the stars through the huge window just behind the headboard. The bed is a twin, made for a growing boy and young man, and surrounded by all of the paraphernalia from his childhood. Sports trophies, photos with his brothers at a lake and the beach and on the front porch. A letterman's jacket for baseball and a secret porn stash under a loose floorboard in his closet that his mom still hasn't found.

He's downstairs on the couch because he refused to sleep on the futon in the guestroom that doubles as Mrs. Wyatt's quilting room and I'm wide awake trying to sort through all the crazy stuff in my head and the even crazier stuff in my heart. It's like I have a constant lyric loop of the mushiest crap running through my head whenever Zane is around and even more when he isn't.

It isn't good. I'm falling for him and he's having a good time with a steady piece of ass on tour.

That's not fair. He's treated me well. He's invested in our friendship...relationship...as much as I have. But we have no labels and I think I might be a girl who needs them.

The stars above me are clear and bright. It's the kind of view you only get out in the country. I envy them their clarity. I could use a little bit of it right now.

The door opens on a sigh and I look over, pulling the covers up to my neck like some old lady in an old movie until I see who it is. I'd know that silhouette anywhere.

ROBIN COVINGTON

"Zane! You can't be in here," I whisper. "You're mom was pretty clear with that she doesn't want any funny stuff going on in her house."

He laughs and tugs his t-shirt off and tosses it on the floor. He's wearing only his boxer briefs and I can see the outline of his hard cock where it tents the fabric.

"Little Bird, my mom knows me. She expects me to get up to 'funny stuff' in her house. She'd be disappointed to find out that I didn't."

I shake my head and laugh even though I know I'm just encouraging him. I sneak a glance over his shoulder towards the door.

"I'm a guest here. I don't want to be disrespectful."

"Well, then we just can't get caught," he drawls, lifting the covers and sliding in beside me in the already too small bed.

He wraps his arms around me and pulls me close, so that I'm draped over his body, nose-to-nose. He grabs my chin and pulls me down into a soft kiss. I respond like I always do, eagerly and encouraging. I run my fingers over his chest, down to his waist where I dig my fingers in and pull him closer. Zane rolls over until I am under him and he starts a slow grind against me, clearly trying to be quiet.

He breaks the kiss, nipping gently at my bottom lip and I chase his tongue, hungry to have him inside me, somehow. Anyway I can get it. I slide my hand down his back and across his ass, tracing the crack with my finger, brushing over his skin the way I know he likes it.

Zane groans and jerks against my touch and the bed squeaks. Loudly. We both freeze.

I let his mouth go but I can feel his hot puffs of air against the wetness on my mouth as we strain our ears for any sign of movement. Nothing.

I relax eventually but gasp when he growls in frustration and pushes himself up and off my body. The blanket goes flying off the bed and onto the floor, quickly followed by all the pillows and then us. A tightened arm around my waist and a flip and we both land in a heap on the pile of bedding.

"Much better," Zane says as he reclaims my kiss. It's hot and wet and dirty in the way that it can only be when you're afraid to get caught. His hand delves under my tank top and finds my nipple, rolling it between his fingers and making me shiver.

I pull out of the kiss and rest my forehead against his as I close my eyes and focus on the river of pleasure running between my breast and my sex. I'm already wet, burning up between my legs where I am rocking against his erection.

"I could come like this," I moan, grinding down harder when his hips buck up under me.

"Could you? You'd could come all over me with your clothes still on?" He asks, his other hand rubbing over the front of my panties. "Goddam, you're soaking wet, baby."

He spears his hands through my hair and pulls me back down to his mouth. This time the kiss is bruising and ferocious and desperate. It's like that first kiss in the Javelin Club but unlike any kiss we've had before. I'm not sure what's happening here but it feels important.

"This is different," he says, as if he can read my thoughts."

"In a bad way?"

He shakes his head. "No. Better. Like I belong here. Like you belong here...with me."

"I do," I answer, pulling back to look into his eyes to gauge his reaction to my words.

"You belong *to* me," he says.

His emphasis is not lost on me and I can only imagine that the shock racing through my body is echoed on my face.

"You know it's true. Don't worry Little Bird..." He puts two of his fingers in my mouth and presses against my tongue. I suck on them, getting them wet and becoming wetter in my sex with every suckling pull. "You've got a claim on me."

I struggle to wrap my head around what he just said but I stop analyzing the minute his hand glides under the back of my panties and his wet fingers press against my asshole. I arch up and against the pressure, panting with the extra adrenaline rush. Zane's head bobs down and I barely feel the rush of air over my bared nipple before it is replaced with the wet, scalding heat of his mouth at the same time his middle digit pushes up inside me.

I cry out and clamp a hand over my mouth as he penetrates me and sucks me to the sharp edge of my orgasm. The initial burn of his intrusion stings in the best way and I push down, encouraging him to continue fucking me with his slow push and retreat.

Another first for me.

Zane hums in approval against my chest as I rock back and forth, up and down. It feels...amazing.

When he releases my breast, I look down and find him staring at me. The twist of his lips is wicked, the twist of his fingers erotic.

"You like that, Em?"

I nod, biting my lip when eases the second one inside me. It stings a little and then it melts into the sweetest pulse of all good things.

"I like seeing your eyes go black, pupils so blown with your pleasure that I can't see any of the emerald. It's fucking hot."

"Come on and fuck me," I beg, lifting my hands to hang on to his shoulders for leverage. "I need it. Need you."

He looks at me like he's memorizing me and I hope he sees what he's doing to me, what he's made me into. A woman who begs her lover to take her whichever way he wants. A woman who is determined to make her own way, find her own path.

"I want to fuck you here," he says while flexing his fingers in my ass. I gasp and writhe against the penetration, wondering if his cock would feel as good. "But not on the floor when I can't let you scream." He nips my bottom lip. "Because I think you'd scream if I took your ass. I've got a feeling that you'd really love it."

"Too much talking, Zane. Just fuck me." I reach up and

tug his hair to make him look me in the eye. "Now."

"You don't ever have to ask me twice."

I lift up far enough to slide my panties and top off and watch as he kicks off his briefs and grabs a condom from the pile of bedding. His cock is thick and hard and my mouth waters as he slides the rubber down and strokes his length as he finds the best position on floor and lies down.

I climb on top and ease myself down on him as he pushes up into me. It's the same as it always is for me. My heartbeat racing, my breathing ragged and my frantic nerves roiling in my gut and under my skin. When my ass touches his thighs I let out a slow breath and wait a moment while I get used to his thickness inside me.

Our eyes lock and I raise up on my knees and slowly lower my body back down. I watch his face in the shadows, the silver moonlight absorbed into the ebony of his hair. He's big and powerful under me but I want to feel that power over me, used against me.

***

Zane

She nudges my hip and I understand her unspoken request and flip us over.

She stretches out, her arms extended high over head, hands clasped together. I suck in a breath at what I think she's asking me to do.

"You want me to hold you down while I fuck you?"

She nods. "Yes. I want to feel you."

I get that. She wants to feel like she belongs to me. I know this because I want her to feel like she belongs to me. Possession. Primal.

"Fine." I lean over her and grasp her wrists with one of my hands. She arches underneath me and my cock slides in deeper with the movement. "Spread your legs wider."

She does, so sweetly that my eyes burn with the emotion that rises up in my chest. Goddam but I don't know what to do with her. She's fucking perfect.

I start to move my hips, thrusting into her and the soft,

broken sounds she makes in the back of her throat make me insane. I know I'm not going to last very long.

"Why does it feel like it's been too long?" I whisper as I push into her, deeper and faster with each stroke.

"You just had me this morning," she half laughs and half moans, her fingers tight where they grip my hand locked around her wrists.

"Too. Fucking Long."

She giggles and then she's coming. The sight of her face in the moonlight, the joy and the pleasure that bubbles up from her chest and from between her lips is too much and I follow her over. The fire deep in my balls, throbbing and sharp as I let how good this feels take over every muscle, every brain cell.

I fall over her and take her own moan as mine with a kiss that is so desperate she must know how deep she's dug into me. My blood pounds in my ears as the last of my orgasm shoots through me and I whimper. I fucking whimper like a slave spread at her feet and begging for any little scrap. Fuck me.

I have never felt this way with a woman. This bone-deep, aching, twenty-four/seven desire to possess her and to let her own me.

It scares the shit out of me and in spite of my earlier semi-confession, I don't think I'm ready to let Emory know her power. It could be dangerous to more than just my sanity. It might be dangerous to my heart.

I fall to her side and drag her against me, letting my breaths even out with hers. Looking up I can see the same view I looked at every night my entire life. The dark sky shot through with thousands of stars. Every single one I made the same wish on: get me off this farm so I can make my music.

"Thank you for coming with me, Little Bird."

She nuzzles into my neck and I can feel her smile against my skin. "You're welcome."

"Was it terrible?" I'm almost afraid to ask because it matters to me that she like this crazy bunch that I have to claim as my family.

"It was..." She pauses while she thinks about her answer and then she amps my curiosity with the "oh hell" she mumbles under her breath before answering. "It was great and awful and awkward and I'm glad I came. You're dad is scary but I think he loves you under all that gruff."

"I think so too." And for the first time in a long time, I do.

"And that's good, right?"

I repeat what I said earlier, "It's the best. It's a place to work on as we figure out the future."

We lie there a while longer and I let the warmth of her body and the citrus scent of her hair wash over me. We are both looking up at the sky when the shooting star falls across the view and out of sight. Freaking sign from somewhere but damn if I know what it means.

"Make a wish, Little Bird," I say, tightening my grip on her waist and drawing her even closer. "But don't tell me what it is or it won't come true."

Minutes pass and she asks, "Did you make a wish, Zane?"

"I did."

"So did I," she murmurs and sinks heavily against my chest, her breath evening out as she slips closer into the sleep.

"I hope we both get what we want."

I settle in to hold her for a while and to think about how I got to this place, full circle but so different and I wonder what tomorrow will bring.

Chapter Seventeen

Zane

The crowd in Atlanta is insane.

I make eye contact with Mac and we both shake our heads at the high energy that is pinging between the band and the audience tonight. I felt it when I opened earlier and it has just been building and building with every song. When Emory and I did our two-song set earlier in the show it was a head rush to actually hear the crowd sing the lyrics along with us. Between the video and the digital downloads, we've gained some fans and it is a bigger thrill than even I imagined.

We end the second encore on the drum and guitar avalanche of sound and then the lights go down for the last time and we all make our way off the stage to the chants of the audience for "one more song". I get off the stage first and grab a towel from a roadie and as soon as Emory is within arm's reach I tug her into the shadows of backstage and kiss her.

She wraps her arms around my neck and opens to my press. I'm sweaty and the hard-on I'm grinding against her could drill through concrete. I can't wait to get her back to the hotel and spend all night inside her. We head back to Nashville tomorrow for a three-show run and then a break for a couple of days. I want to spend the time off with Emory but I haven't found a minute to ask her.

Too many days on the road, too many early morning PR events and I've been in interviews all morning with the band or with Emory and I'm beat. But its nothing that a little one-on-one time with Emory can't fix.

It feels like forever since the night at my parent's house. She was so sweet as I fucked her on the floor, giving me everything she had and I realized as her wet heat squeezed me that I want it all. I want her. I want her in my bed and in my life. I want the labels.

My wish on that star was for her. Just her.

I'm looking forward to the time I will have to figure out exactly what that means for both of us. It won't be easy with my career and whatever she decides to do with her talent but I think we've got a better shot than most. Now, I just need to see if she's on the same page.

"Is that a guitar in your pocket or are you just happy to see me?" She jokes as we break apart.

"I can't help it. You plus the crowd and the music and I just want to get you naked and under me as soon as possible," I groan as I press a kiss against the sweaty skin on her neck. Her hands insinuate themselves under the hem of my shirt and I gasp at the sensation of her fingers gliding over my overly sensitized skin. She kisses along my jaw, nipping under my chin with little bites that make me shiver. I grab her ass, haul her closer and she raises her legs to climb me like a tree.

"As much as I like the porno encore you two have going on here, Kit wants you both in the green room," Mac's voice breaks through my haze of music–induced lust and I spin to shield Emory from his gaze. "Now."

"What the hell?" I ask and he just shrugs and gives me the "what-the-fuck-do-I-know" look.

"Come on," Emory grabs my hand and drags me through the backstage area. "The sooner we get this done, the sooner we can go back to the hotel."

I release her hand and grab her by the waist, dragging her back against me so I can still press kisses against her neck as we walk.

"I think I created a sex monster," I joke as she sneaks a hand back to grab my ass.

"Are you complaining?"

"Fuck no!" I laugh, letting her go when we reach the

threshold of the green room. Everyone knows we're together but there is a place and time. Backstage after a show is always a yes. At a meeting called by your boss and your girlfriend's big sister is always a no.

We walk into the room and the wall of sound by thirty people screaming, "congratulations" makes us both stumble backwards. I reach for Emory and steady her on her high-heeled boots.

"What the hell?"

Kit is standing in the middle of the crowd with her manager, Paul Brandt and my agent, Andrew Locke. Mac stands beside her, his big hands holding a large framed item.

A gold album.

"Oh my God," Emory says and I look down to see her place her hand over her mouth, eyes wide with shock. "Oh my God."

Kit steps forward and everyone in the room gets quiet. "Emory and Zane. Congratulations, your single, *Lies and Love*, has gone gold!"

Flashes go off and I realize that the tour photographer is here capturing every moment. Everyone in the room starts yelling again and it takes a few moments for Kit to get them to shut up.

"This is an amazing accomplishment and the only thing that could possibly make it better is the fact that you have three offers on the table from three of the largest labels in the business." She gets choked up and fans her face with a hand as she takes a few second to pull herself together. "It is so well-deserved. Congratulations!"

The next minute the hoard of people rush towards us and we are hugged and kissed within an inch of our lives. Everyone is happy for us and many have tears in their eyes. They all get it. This business is hard and we just jumped a big hurdle. This is huge. I look for Emory but she's wrapped up in the arms of her big sister and Sandra. Our eyes meet across the crowd and I smile at her. She mouths "fuck yeah" and I laugh.

Emory gets me and I know just how lucky I am.

Mac looms in front of me and we fist bump before he hands over the framed record. I just stare at it, not quite believing what I am seeing.

"That's fucking awesome, man," he says. "You and Emory *killed* it."

I nod, a grin finally replacing the goofy look of shock I know I had on my face. "I can't believe it. This is...unbelievable."

"Well, *believe it* dumbass because you've got a decision to make about what label you're going to sign with so that you can start on your plan for world domination."

My plan. All that hard work. Years of writing songs for other people. Years of gigs in shitty bars and hand selling my stuff out of the back of my car. The plan worked. Halle-fucking-lujah.

"You are the luckiest bastard on the planet. You've got the hit, the contract and the girl," he says.

I look over at Emory and remember last night in my childhood bed. He's more right than he knows. "I should go buy a lottery ticket."

"You're not going anywhere until we talk about these contract offers." Andrew appears at my elbows and waves a leather binder full of papers in my face. "I got the first one about an hour after the news about the gold record hit the industry pipeline. By the time the third one rolled in, I booked a flight for Atlanta."

"Is this really happening?" I ask, wondering if I need to pinch myself.

"It's happening," Emory says as she wraps her arms around my neck and kisses me. Somebody takes the gold record out of my hand so I can hold her tight and kiss her back. She's happy and hungry and playful as she breaks it off with a tiny nip teeth on my bottom lip. "Can you believe it? This is crazy."

"It's about to get crazier," Kit says. "You guys want to take this into my dressing room and see what's on the table?"

I lean down and whisper against Emory's ear. "Come on Little Bird, let's get this over with and then I'll show you how I like to celebrate."

She shivers against me, her fingers digging into my side as we follow her sister down the hallway and into the quiet of her dressing room.

"Emory, I know you don't have an agent yet so Paul is here to advise you if that's okay," Kit says as soon as the door is closed. From her place at my side on the couch, Emory nods.

"That would be great. Thank you Paul."

"You bet kiddo," Paul smiles and lowers his big frame into a chair next to us.

"We have three offers on the table," Andrew begins and withdraws a pile of papers from his leather binder. "One from Tribeca Media, one from Roadtrip Records, and one from Radio 360. All are 360 offers with the difference being the amount of creative control."

He hands the papers to us and Emory and I take them. I look down and scan the first one and then the second and third. I look up at Andrew, confused.

"These deals are for a group. They aren't solo deals." Andrew looks at me like I have a third eye so I clarify. "We were looking for a solo deal, right?"

He glances at Emory and looks embarrassed. "Zane, the gold record was for the work you did together. Everyone loves the songs the two of you write. They want to see you perform *as a group*."

I stand up and drop the papers on the table. I'm shaking all over, vibrating with disappointment and anger. It's like whiplash when I was so high just few minutes earlier.

"Andrew, this thing was just for fun. Exposure. It was just fooling around." I just struggle with the words I need to express my outrage. It's hard to believe that I write songs for a living. "I did not work my ass off to *settle* for being part of a duo. Fuck that."

"Wow. I had no idea. I'm flattered you wasted your time

with me at all." Emory fumes beside me, her green eyes on fire with her anger and her body rigid. I can also see the hurt but I don't know what she expected. This isn't anything we ever talked about. I never knew she wanted it.

"Godammit Emory, you knew what I wanted. I never hid it from you. We never talked about making this permanent. Don't act like I broke some big fucking pinky swear with you."

"I'm sorry. I thought we were building something together here."

"Sleeping together and my career are two very separate things. If you weren't nineteen you would have realized that."

Emory reels back from words and the look of hurt on her face. I replay what I said and too late I realize just how ugly they were.

"Wait. Wait. I didn't mean that. I'm sorry."

"The part about fucking me or the part about playing music with me?"

"Whoa. Time out." Kit jumps up and wedges in between us. "You guys are tired and there's a lot of shit to absorb here. Why don't you go back to the hotel, get a shower, food and we can regroup?"

She looks at Andrew and Paul and they both nod in agreement.

"It doesn't matter. I'm never going to sign those papers." I brush past Emory and head for the door. I put a hand on the doorknob and turn to direct my last comment to Andrew. "I hired you to get me a solo deal. I worked my ass off for a solo deal. Get me one."

***

I still can't believe how fucked up this is.

I pace my room, head still wet from the shower, towel around my waist and a second beer in my hand. Over two hours to fume and think and I'm still pissed. Molten lava pissed. I can't believe that I worked for all that time and this is how I get a deal.

Three deals.

My gut clenches when I think of how it went down with Emory. I didn't mean to hurt her, I would never deliberately make her feel so shitty. I was pissed and the words just flew out before I even thought about them. I need to go find her and talk to her without a gazillion other people in the room and make her understand that our being together has nothing to do with business.

They are separate. At least they always were for me.

I reach for my cellphone to call her. She could be in her room or with Kit plotting the best way to string me up by my balls. I thumb across the screen to make the call when someone knocks at my door. I walk over to it, hoping that it's Emory and we can work this out. I open the door and the person standing in the hallway is not who I expected.

Not at all.

"Hey Zane. You busy?" Maureen Richards walks her ass right past me and into my hotel room. She always dresses to impress and to get you undressed and tonight is a stellar entry. Dark brown, form-fitting and very short. Her breasts are on partial display and her legs end in the kind of heels you usually see propped up on some guy's shoulder in a porno.

This isn't her office wear. This is what she puts on when she hits the club and wants to use all of her assets to get an artist to sign on the dotted line.

It almost worked on me.

"Not a good time Maureen," I say, turning to face her as she paces around my room. She picks up my beer and takes a sip and eye fucks me so hard that I wonder if I should get a condom. I'll have to adjust my towel if my dick notices anymore.

"I heard that it was a great day for you Zane. Congratulations."

"Thanks. I appreciate it." I wave my phone at her. "I was making a call when you showed up."

"You're not accepting those offers from Tribeca, Roadtrip, and Radio 360 are you?" She walks towards me but stops at the desk wedged behind the sofa. She places her bag on the tabletop and reaches inside, producing a folder full of papers. She holds it out to me and when I hesitate, she gives it an extra wave. "It's not going to bite you, Zane. Read it."

I watch her closely. Maureen never has only one agenda. It's why I avoided getting in her bed. She's always playing some angle and I didn't want a sex life that felt like a chess match. I take a step forward and put my phone down on the desk and take the papers. I open the folder and skim the pages, sighing heavily when I see what she's done.

"It's a 360 deal that gives you complete creative control. Solo. None of that duo shit the other ones tried to sell you," she says, her voice low with a hint of seduction on every single syllable. Maureen has me by the balls and she knows it. "You are going to be fucking huge and I want to be the one to help you get there."

"You or Waterworld Media?"

She shrugs and smiles, moving close enough to allow her to rub a fingertip over the edge of my towel. "I plan to take a personal interest in your career."

"Really? You weren't that interested in signing me before. Where was this deal six months ago?"

"That was six months ago." I feel her finger move inside the towel and stroke against the flesh of my hip. My cock perks up to applaud the additional offer that is obviously on the table. "Dump the teenager and take the career opportunity you worked your ass off for, Zane. All the rest of it extra perks for a job well done."

"Don't fucking talk about Emory."

"Oh, don't tell me its' gotten serious. Are you taking her to prom? Giving her your class ring?"

"Don't be a bitch."

"You want me to be a bitch, Zane, That's how I got you this amazing fucking deal." Maureen removes her hand from my crotch and trails it up my bare chest, resting the palm against my heart. Right now it is pounding like Mac's drum kit and I curse the fact that she knows she has my interest. "You don't want to throw this away because you're afraid to hurt the feelings of a girl you've been screwing for a few weeks. You really don't."

I don't agree with anything she said about Emory but it is an enticing offer.

All of my dreams laid out on a platter.

The Devil doesn't have to do anything but dress up as your wildest wish to get your soul.

"Fuck me," I breathe out on a sigh, my eyes closed tight.

"All you have to do is ask," she says and then her mouth is on mine.

I open my lips and she tastes of mint gum and the whisky she must have had down in the bar. Maureen is a gorgeous woman, experienced and she knows how to kiss a man to get a response so when she moves in and presses her body against me, I wrap my hand around the back of her neck to keep her in the place where I can control the kiss.

She immediately dives a hand underneath my towel and her fingers stroking my cock feels good. I'm a guy, so any hand on my dick that isn't mine feels good. But this doesn't feel...right.

Maureen is not Emory. She doesn't smell like sunshine and citrus. She's not tall enough so our bodies don't fit together like a perfect puzzle. There's product in her hair so the strands do not feel like icy silk against my skin. She doesn't make the sound in the back of her throat that makes me shiver.

She's not Emory.

And I want Emory.

I pull away from the kiss so abruptly that Maureen stumbles and has to steady herself against the desk. She looks up at me confused and off balance, lipstick smeared until something behind me catches her eye and she transfers her focus to it.

I turn to see what she's looking at and I know.

I know just what a huge fucking mistake I've made.

Emory is there for a split second and if I thought the words I said earlier hurt her, the expression on her face right now tells me that was paper scratch compared to the knife I just put in her back.

Chapter Eighteen

Emory

Oh fuck no.

I back out of the room like my ass is on fire. There is no reason for me to stay since the image of Zane with his towel practically falling off his body and that bitches lipstick smeared all over his mouth is permanently burned on my brain. I take off down the hallway, digging my keycard out of my pocket and head to my room.

"Em, wait!"

I keep walking, refusing to look back at him. I blink my eyes, forcing back the tears I know are just waiting for the chance to roll down my cheeks. I will not cry in front of him or that woman. Never. I dig in my pocket for my keycard as I approach my room.

"Em. Stop. Let's talk about this."

Zane grabs my arm and I wrench it away, my own momentum bashing me into my door with a loud thud.

"Don't fucking touch me, Zane," I growl at him as the door across the hall opens and Kit comes out into the hallway. I take a quick glance around and realize that half the band is witnessing my humiliation, my broken heart. "I am such a fucking idiot."

"No. No, you're not," he say, his voice gentle and pleading. It's like he thinks I won't make a scene if he talks sweet to me. I don't want to make a scene but he has lost his mind if he thinks I'm just going off quietly into the night.

I wave a hand over at where Maureen stands with smug look on her face. I hate her so much right now that I could do some damage if she got close enough.

"Yes, I am. I'm an idiot because I thought the problem was the contract for a duo when the real problem was your fear that you might have to pass up USDA primetime pussy somewhere else if you stayed with me."

"Emory!" Kit gasps, the shock in her voice clearly displayed on her face. "What the hell are you talking about?"

I laugh. It's broken and bitter and feels like glass in my throat. "I went to his room to talk this out and he's getting his new contract offer via the mouth-to-mouth method from this bitch. I shouldn't have been surprised. She's been chasing his tail forever and now she's going to get it."

"Emory, I think you need to think about this with your head and not your heart. Once you have more life experience, you'll understand that this is how business is sometimes. It's not personal," Maureen says, her tone so smooth, I wonder if she practices it in the mirror.

I ignore her and look at Zane. "It felt personal to me. Was I wrong?"

He has the good grace to look away, an embarrassed flush on his cheeks. When he finally returns my gaze, his eyes are sad and I fight the urge to make him feel better. Fuck him.

"I don't..." he stammers out his answer as his fingers run through his hair in agitation. "I fucking don't know. I need to think..."

"Take all the time you need because I think I got my answer loud and clear. I'm not making records with you and I'm not fucking you. We're done. You can take your contract with Maureen and sell a gazillion records, see if I care."

But I do care and anyone who can hear how my voice is shaking knows it. Zane sure does and he moves to touch me but I flinch away.

"I don't want *us* to be over," he pleads.

"We. Are. Over." I say with conviction that is so hard it breaks what's left of my heart into a million pieces. "I got carried away and thought that what we had was *more* than the music. I was wrong."

We stare at each other for a several long moments. I break eye contact when I know that he's got nothing to offer me that will make this alright.

"Okay let's get this out of the hallway," Kit says and grabs me by the arm and shoves me in her room. She pauses on the threshold and barks out orders. "Maureen get the hell off my floor. I have the whole thing booked for tonight. Zane put some clothes on."

I flop down on the couch and lean over to open the mini-fridge. Grabbing a beer, I pop the top and take a deep gulp. When I look up, Kit is frowning at me.

"What?"

"Those were some pretty harsh words out there."

"I would have said more but I didn't want to lose my shit and cry in front of that awful woman." I put my beer down on the table and cover my face with my hands.

I can feel the tears seeping in between my fingers and dropping onto my knees. Kit's arms wrap around me and I let it all go. She sits there beside me and takes it like only big sister can and I am grateful for her.

"I'm so embarrassed," I say, in between my attempts to get my breathing under control.

"Don't ever be embarrassed because you fell in love. You can hurt and curse it and regret it but don't ever be ashamed," Kit murmurs against my hair. "He loves you. The stupid idiot just doesn't realize it."

I pull away from her, shaking my head as I dry my eyes. "No. No. You can't say stuff like that. I can't have hope about this. I need to see it for what it is and let it go."

"And what is it?"

"It's the end of an affair. A fling. Yes, it was intense and I invested more of myself in it than I should have but now it's over. I'm not what he wants on the stage with him or in his life. I need to accept it."

She looks mulish and like she wants to argue with me but she holds it in.

I understand the way it is. The entire situation is as clear to me as crystal and I can see that I have no place in it.

"Kit, he's worked hard for a solo deal and I think it's unrealistic for me to expect that I can come along and change that. He's a determined man and if he really wanted me, he would have fought harder but he didn't. In fact, he not only ran to another record deal but lined up another woman for his bed. To ignore that would make me either very stupid or crazy. " I sigh and face the rest of my truth. "For him the music and a relationship are two separate things. It's not for me. I wrote those lyrics for him, with him because I love him. For me it's the whole package. I can't just accept half of it and be happy."

"But will you be happy without any of it?"

"I think I have to be."

Chapter Nineteen

Zane

"You are such a dick."

I look up from my spot on the couch where I'm playing a ninja video game to see Mateo standing behind me. He drops his messenger bag to the floor and throws his keys on the table before going to the fridge to grab two beers. He hops the couch and lands with a thud, sloshing a little bit of the brew on his jeans before handing one over to me.

I take it and swallow down a mouthful of the cold beverage. It slides down smooth and then settles around the cold lump lying in the pit of my stomach. On the screen my character is getting his ass kicked all over the place. I don't really care. His beat down is the perfect demonstration of how I feel at the moment. It's the same thing I've felt since Emory left me in that hallway with my junk half hanging out of that stupid towel.

"You're getting killed, man," Mateo says, nodding towards the TV screen.

"I don't care." I throw the controller at the coffee table and watch as it bounces off and disappears. I hear a thump as it hits the floor and decide to leave it.

"For a guy who has an amazing contract just waiting for your signature, you sure are acting like an asshole." Mateo raises his palm and smacks himself on the forehead. "That's right! You haven't signed the fucking amazing contract sitting on the table yet. Instead you're lying on the couch and losing against imaginary characters in a stupid ninja game that only twelve year olds play."

"I can't sign it, Mateo. I just can't"

"Why? Because it isn't what you want? What does Andrew say about it?"

I take another sip of beer and settle back against the cushions. "He says it's a great deal because it is. They are all stellar deals and I would be crazy to turn any of them down."

"So, what's the problem?"

I know he knows the answer but he's going to bug me until I talk about it.

"I want to sign the one with Emory," I say for the first time out loud and it feels really good and shitty at the same time because I know it is too little , too late. I hurt her so badly. The look on her face in the hallway is etched on my aching heart with a burning coal. "I went to sign the deal from Waterworld. I had my pen on the fucking paper and I couldn't do it because I can't imagine doing this without her. I don't know when it happened but she became part of the plan…fuck, she's bigger than the plan." I stand and start to pace. This whole thing has me wired tighter than a newly tuned piano. "And she won't talk to me. She won't answer her phone. I even went to the loft and she's not there so I drove out to Max and Kit's place and they wouldn't even let me on the porch."

"I know. Max was torn between coming over here to talk and jerking a knot in your ass. He is pissed and worried about you."

"I'm pissed at me too." I think back to the day in Atlanta when I screwed all this up. It was only a day ago but it feels like forever. "I panicked and said terrible things that I don't mean and then I kissed Maureen…" That thought makes me so angry at myself that I clench my fists to keep from punching the wall. "I can't stand the thought of never being with Emory again. It's got me by the balls, man. I love her and she hates me."

"Well then get her back." He looks at me like it's the easiest thing in the world. Like I can just snap my fingers and it will be like my stupidity never happened. I stare at him long enough that he says it again, slowly and with precise pronunciation. "Got. Get. Her. Back."

"I have no idea how to do that, Mateo. If I knew, I would be doing it."

"Who are you?' He plops the beer down on the table and stands cutting around the table to get within reach to poke my chest. "Seriously, who the fuck are you?"

"I don't know," I say, knowing that it is the truth.

"Where's the guy who ate mustard sandwiches when he used his scholarship money to buy a new guitar? Where's the asshole who dragged me to bars so dangerous that he had to perform behind a wire cage? Where's the man who wrote two top ten songs before he turned fucking twenty years old?" He throws his hands up in the air in disgust. "You'll do all of that for a dream but you won't fight for the woman you say you love? I ask it again: who the fuck are you?"

I stare at him as his words hit me in the gut like a sucker punch.

"You're right. But how do I do that when I can't get her to talk to me?"

"If you love her then there's only one real solution, Zane."

"Tell me. I'll do it." I am *this close* to begging and he knows it but he takes pity on me and doesn't make me wait too long.

"You need to grovel. On your knees and beg her to take you back. In public. You need to make a total ass of yourself." He smiles and delivers the singer like only a best friend can. "That should easy for you."

Chapter Twenty

Emory

"Your Daddy would be so proud of you tonight," Mama says.

She glances at Kit standing over near the vanity in my dressing room of the Grand Ole Opry. Mama's expression turns to one of regret and apology when she realizes that references to our wayward, bigamist daddy might be a sore spot with my half-sister. But I can't even feel the full extent of the sympathy I should because I feel like I'm going blow chunks all over the "Cousin Minnie Pearl" dressing room.

"Kit..." Mama reaches out a hand to the woman I now consider a sister and more importantly, a friend. "I'm sorry to bring up hard memories for you. Your daddy...well he left us with a mess, didn't he?"

Kit glances at me and the look passing between us tells me that no matter how far we've come there's still a few bridges we need to cross. All I know is that if we want to do it then maybe we can become the family we both want. She nods at me like she understands what's rolling around in my head and then she reaches out and grabs Mama's hand before answering.

"Mrs. Cabell, I think we both loved him and I understand that he needed to find some happiness. He would want us to be family and share those memories."

Mama tears up immediately, her lashes blinking rapidly as she tries to force back the waterworks. Her voice is a little wobbly but strong. "Kit, I think you're right and I'd like that. Very much...but only if you call me Ruthanne."

Wow. What a difference a year makes. Even if everything else in my life went to hell, at least I've got this. A new beginning. A new family.

I step forward and we all mush into one of those sappy Hallmark movie group hugs where we all end up sniffling and awkwardly trying to maintain some sort of grip on the other two. Kit pulls out first and her eyebrows shoot up when she gets a look at my face. She shoves me towards my dressing table in the corner.

"Emory, you need to fix your eye makeup and stop bawling or you won't be able to sing."

I obey her instruction and balk when I see the damage our little moment caused. Frankenstein's Bride had more color in her cheeks than I do and fewer bags under eyes. Earlier, Kit had sent in her makeup artist to cover the evidence of all the crying I'd done over the last few days and while I can reapply the concealer, nothing will cover-up the hurt that swims in my eyes.

Wrecked. Ravaged. That pain is all my eyes and Maybelline hasn't made the stuff that can hide it. I pick up the case left by the makeup artist for touch-ups and start to fix the mess. I'm grateful to have something to do when Mama starts talking.

"Emory, I was hoping to meet Zane before your performance tonight."

I cut a glance at Kit and she winces at the question. I haven't really filled my mother in on all of the details of what happened between us. I know there are some daughters who tell their mama everything but I'm not that girl. I'm built like my mama in that respect but where she bottles stuff up and lets it eat at her, I put it all in my music.

So tonight I'm the best damn performer in the universe and I should get an Oscar. As far as anyone knows, including mama, the only thing wrong with me is a rookie case of nerves.

I briefly lock eyes with Kit in the mirror before returning my gaze to my task. "Mama, you'll meet him tonight. He's just giving us some space to enjoy my first night at the Opry together."

"Emory got to pick her dressing room Ruthanne and she told me that you were a big Minnie Pearl fan," Kit says and turns the conversation over to a topic that doesn't make it hard for me to breathe.

Mama nods happily. "I just loved to watch her on Hee-Haw. I grew up listening to her on the old radio shows and I never in a million years thought my daughter would be playing on the same stage."

"When I played here for the first time, I thought I was going to fall down my knees were shaking so much," Kit says.

"Well, it must run in the family because if I don't fall down it will be a miracle," I say and send up a silent prayer that I don't end up on my knees in front of the live and television audience. It would memorable for all the wrong reasons.

Two quick raps on the door and just seconds after I tell whoever it is to come in, Max sticks his head inside and smiles. "Okay, they're giving you the ten minute signal so I thought I'd come get Mrs. Cabell and take her out to her seat."

"Max, that would be awesome," I walk over to Mama and pull her into a hug and kiss her cheek before pushing her towards my sister's fiancée. "I want you to clap really loud for me, okay?"

She nods and blows me a kiss as she walks away and I think I see her pull another one of the never-ending supply of tissues out of her purse and dab at her eyes as the door closes behind them. In the relative silence of the dressing room I close my eyes, take a deep breath, and slowly exhale, willing the tension that I feel creeping into my limbs to hit the road.

"You okay?" Kit asks and I open my eyes and look at her. What the hell am I supposed to say to that? It's like I'm split in two. One-half decimated by the ache in my heart and the other beyond excited that I am going to stand up in front of these people on the stage I dreamed about my whole life.

The rock and the hard place are looking really good right now.

I'm spared having to answer by another, sharper knock on the door and the voice of one of the assistants to somebody-who-makes-the-show-happen is loud and firm even through the heavy wood.

"Ms. Cabell, I need you stage right to get set-up with your monitor."

I walk over and open the door, smiling at the thirty-something woman holding an iPad and wearing a blue tooth headset. She grins back, clearly pleased that I'm ready to go.

"Excellent! I was hoping I wouldn't have to coax you out of the bathroom and slip you a barf bag like some other people I know," she jokes while sliding a look in Kit's direction.

"Hey, it was only that one time, Susan," Kit protests, walking over with my guitar in her hand. "And, for the record I didn't actually use the bag until *after* the show."

"Did you really throw up after your first-time performing at the Opry?" I ask Kit, unable to believe that my big sister, the consummate performer, ever had to deal with a case of the nerves.

"I confess to being a little green around the gills but I kept my dinner down before, during and after the show."

"I like my story better," Susan answers, giving me the "come on" gesture as she heads down the hallway. "We need to get moving."

I follow behind her trying to return the smiles of the people I pass as I make my way to backstage. My stomach is doing backflips and my heart is pounding but mingled equally with the nervousness is pure excitement. I dreamed about this moment and now it is here. Even heartache can't completely kill the moment

We turn a corner and there it is: the stage of the Grand Ole Opry. Bathed in lights I have a clear view of the performers and the full-house audience just beyond. The music is loud, the notes vibrating under my feet as the current band plays in perfect sync. It is exhilarating and terrifying at the same time, two sides of a coin.

"Wow," I say on a whoosh of an exhale, caught somewhere between and laugh and gasp. "This is..."

"I know. The Mother Church is an awesome sight isn't it?" Kit murmurs beside me, her hand at my back a steadying touchstone.

"Hey."

I hear his smooth, sexy-as-sin voice and curse that he still has the power to make my stomach flip-flop with excitement. I never thought I was one of those girls who go for the bad boy but when they wrap themselves up in a sweet candy coating, I'm a goner. Zane was a sugar rush and now all I'm left with is a bellyache.

I fell hard for Zane. I'm just glad I never told him. Just how big a fool I am remains my own little secret.

"Hey," I answer, proud that my voice remains steady as I turn to look at him.

He looks so good, white v-neck t-shirt, black leather pants and boots. His tats are on his muscled forearms and biceps, his dark hair down and brushing his shoulders. The cruelest part is the dark stubble in his goatee and the memory of how good it felt against my skin. He's staring right at me and I know he can see the heat that crawls over my skin. He knows me because I let him in. I hate it.

"You look beautiful," he says and the truth of it in his eyes makes me tear up. I can't answer him and just shake my head, grateful when the sound techs come over to hook us up with our in-ear monitors.

I know he cares about me. I know he thinks I'm beautiful. That's what makes this so hard; because I saw what we could have been and it felt real. I just can't get the sight of him in Miranda's arms out of my head where it replays like a marathon of grisly *Law and Order* episodes. He told me what he was about from the beginning and I just didn't believe him. My first hard lesson learned in this big city. It won't be my last heartbreak but the scar from this cut will be hard to ignore or forget. That's probably a good thing. It will serve as a warning to me in the future.

The techs finish their work and I look anywhere but at him. I can feel his eyes on me and when I see him step forward in my peripheral vision I step back. I need to perform and if Zane touches me, I'll never get through it.

"Little Bird," he murmurs.

"Zane. Don't," I answer, my voice sharper than even I expected. I can feel his physical retereat.

"Hey, guys," Kit steps between us, her hands resting on our shoulders. "This is a big night, your first on the Opry stage. I know things aren't right between the two of you but you need to forget it for the next ten minutes. Three songs. One set. Your problems will be waiting for you when you get off the stage. You wrote an incredible song and the people in those seats want to hear you sing it. Don't disappoint them and don't steal this moment from yourselves."

I sneak a peek at Zane, we lock eyes and a lifetime of shit passes between us in those few seconds. What could have been. What we had. It all swirls in the space we can either leave gaping between us or close with one word. I don't have that word; I have no idea what he could say to make me believe him again. I have no idea what but Zane does.

"It's just the music Emory. Let it do the talking tonight." His dark eyes are intense, hot. It's like we're back in that club the first night we kissed and I feel the heat deep in my marrow. The music and this man are so tied up together for me and I have no hope of separating them right now in the wings of the Opry stage.

"Kit's right. Our shit will still be here when this is over and we can figure it out then. I don't want to miss this moment," I say as I place the strap of my guitar over my shoulders and turn away from him and face the stage. I'm a performer and that means that I will go out there and do what I need to do.

The band currently on stage finishes their set and bows to applause of the audience and then I watch as Kit is announced and walks out on the stage to introduce us. And then it is "go" time and I step out onto the stage, fighting the urge to look back at Zane.

Chapter Twenty-One

Zane

The show must fucking go on.

I walk onto the Opry stage, close on Emory's heels with a smile plastered on my face. I've played when I was sick, hung over, and sleep-deprived. I can do this. Three songs. Ten minutes and the press junket after the show and then we get two days off.

Two days for me to initiate the plan get her back. I still have no idea what I'm going to do but I need to make it happen soon so I can sleep, so I can breathe again. We aren't done with the tour for six more weeks and if I fail, I don't know how I'm going to get through it with Emory so close but so far away.

The audience is still applauding and we both pause in front of the microphones to acknowledge the cheers and whistles. The lights are harsh but she shines under them, her golden hair in curls that form a halo around her beautiful face. The sweet slope of her shoulder, the spot I love to caress with my mouth, is exposed by her strapless top and the knowledge that I will never touch her there again forces me to take a sharp breath against the pain in my chest.

I step up and speak to the crowd, just like we rehearsed.

"Thanks so much for having us here tonight. What a crazy ride it has been for both of us. We never thought it would bring us here but we are so grateful. Thank you."

I look at Emory and she is poised, her hand hovering over the strings of her guitar as she waits for the drummer to count off. Our eyes meet for the briefest of moments before her clear voice spins out like gold with the melancholy song.

"Don't look back. There's nothing here for you to see. Whatever we had, whatever we made is lost. No rescue. No hope of revival. The unknown is the only thing worth hoping for since you walked away."

I close my eyes, cursing the day we wrote the lyrics. I thought I had some idea of what the words meant but I had no idea. It was like my subconscious saw the future and put the words on the page that night to torture me now.

I take up the song on the second half of the first verse.

"I saw you tonight and you looked right through me. You've moved on but I'm stuck in our past with no one to blame but myself. Foolish pride. Stupid weakness. Hoping you'll take pity on me."

A few bars and the chorus starts and I open my mouth to take up the harmony but I freeze, my throat tight. Emory continues on for two more bars, falters, and then turns to me, her eyes searching. Whatever she sees in my face makes her own voice waver, the words trailing off with the rest of the band as they realize that I have lost my mind.

The silence in such a large, packed place is complete and unsettling. Past the stage lights, I see the audience shift in their seats and the questioning looks passing between them as the moments stretch out.

"Zane," Emory says, stepping close to look at me. Everything about her stance is concerned but wary. I don't blame her. I don't know if I trust myself at this moment but I know what I need to do.

"Emory," I say, stopping when I realize don't really know how to start. I break eye contact with her and start to speak into the microphone again, unsure about what I'm going to say. Her blue eyes search my face and I ache to reach out and touch her but that won't fix this. Sex, kisses, attraction…that isn't the problem. I know what I need to do to get anywhere close to making this right. I turn from her and face the crowd.

"Ladies and gentlemen, I've spent most of my life hoping that I would be invited to play on this stage and this moment..." I take a deep breath when my words catch in my throat. "...this moment is a dream come true. Or it should be. But I realize that I'm standing here with everything I always thought I wanted and all I can think is that I did the wrong thing to the right girl."

I ignore the ripple of surprise that passes through the audience and turn to look at Emory. She's completely still, her eyes huge and the pale skin of her cheeks flushed with the blush that gives away her high emotion. Her long fingers grip the neck of her guitar with a white-knuckle ferocity.

"Little Bird, you have fascinated me since the first moment I met you because I knew you were special. Every second we've spent together has been the most amazing time of my life. It's never been just the music between us. The songs we've written are so good because of what we feel about each other."

She scoffs at my words, her eyes flashing with all the hurt and anger *I* put there.

"And how do we feel about each other Zane?"

"I love you and I know you love me."

I ignore the murmurings of the crowd listening to our every word and keep my focus on her.

"No. I don't."

"Yes. You do."

"I don't like you," she says, the stubborn tilt of her chin trembling a bit with her emotion.

"That's okay because I don't like me either." I reach out and grab her hand, tugging her closer. "Baby, I messed up. I was a coward and I hurt you because I was afraid to change my stupid plan for something different. Something better. But I *know* that you are the best thing that has ever happened to me or will ever happen to me. I want to live with you, love you, and make music together. Please give me another chance."

"Those are just words Zane," she says, her eyes glossy with her tears and her lip trembles but she forces out the next sentence and cuts me to the quick. "It's just the music. We got wrapped up in the music and now we just need to let it go."

There's a special kind of hell when you have your own words thrown back at you. I am there right now.

"We got wrapped up in *our* music. Not the notes we wrote down and recorded in the studio but the music that comes to life when you and I touch. When I kiss you it's like a damn symphony starts playing in my head. When we make love it's the universe's perfect melody." I take a deep breath, my own emotions choking me as I realize this might not work. I might have fucked this up beyond repair. "I love you and I need you. I need you in my bed, in my life and with me here on the stage. Nothing about this means anything if I don't have you."

"What about your plan?" She asks as a tear slides down her cheek and hangs like a perfect diamond on her chin.

I reach up and brush it away and when she doesn't reject my touch I walk forward as close I can get and cup her face in my hands.

"*You* are my plan. You've always been the plan. I just didn't know it yet."

Not a fucking sound fills the longest thirty seconds of my life as I wait to hear her answer. Her expression is full of pain and confusion and I have no idea what she's thinking. I can't wait. I give her all I've got.

"I love you Emory Cabell. When we saw that shooting star, *you* are what I wished for. Not contracts or big tours. Not even a new song. Just you."

Two big fat tears spill down her cheeks and my stomach falls into my boots because making a girl cry on the Grand Ole Opry stage can't be a good thing. But Emory surprises me. Like she always does.

"I love you too Zane."

The microphone picks up her whisper and the audience goes nuts. I ignore all of the applause and cheers and pull her to me, kissing her with relief and something that has to be joy.

Her lips are warm and soft and open to me at the first

brush of my tongue against them. I dive in, wanting to claim her promise laden words before she can change her mind. My fingers slide into the silken fall of her hair and I pull her even closer, shoving our guitars to the side as we come together for our first kiss as lovers. The best kiss.

I can already hear the song I'm going to write about this. It will go fucking platinum.

I pull back from the kiss but Emory isn't done. She grabs my t-shirt in her fists and drags me back down to her mouth and the audience goes even crazier. Whistles. Hoots. Foot stomps. It is pandemonium. I get in a couple of quick swipes of my tongue before our laughter makes us break the kiss. I look beyond the footlights and everyone is on their feet as the band starts the beginning of *Lies and Love*, the opening beats fast and furious.

I turn back to look at Emory and she's grinning and giving me *those* eyes. The ones that tell me she's going to jump my bones the minute she can get me to a private, horizontal place. But this time there's something more in her gaze...or maybe I'm finally recognizing what else was there all along.

"Never stop looking at me like that," I say, hoping she remembers when I said something similar but very different.

She does. Emory laughs and steps back, mimicking my movements as we get our guitars in position to play.

"Why?" She asks.

"Because I want *everyone* to know just how much I love you."

If you loved REDEMPTION, continue with the rest of the Nashville Nights series...

TEMPTATION

She needs to be good.

At sixteen, Kit ditched her crappy life and moved to Nashville with only $200, her guitar, and a notebook full of songs. She hit it big, but five years of living like a rock star plus a stint in rehab has killed any good will she had with her label. The suits have ordered Kit to shape up or ship out of the limelight. The last thing she needs is a hot, sexy distraction with a sinful smile.

He doesn't know the meaning of the word.

Max Butler is as far from a celebrity as you can get and he likes it that way. A Nashville firefighter, he's living the single life with a revolving door of parties, friends, and a different woman in his bed every night. When his normal life suddenly collides with the girl on his favorite Rolling Stone cover, he sees the perfect chance to fulfill his ultimate fantasy and see just how bad Kit can be.

Sometimes bad is so very good.

With three weeks until Kit leaves for her big tour, Max promises to give her a break from being the good girl--no strings attached. But when hot days lead to sultry nights, the lines get blurred and suddenly three weeks of bad might not be good enough.

Buy it on the TEMPTATION page: http://robincovingtonromance.com/books/nashville-nights-series/temptation/.

SALVATION

Letting go never felt so good.

Carlisle Queen is dying and no one knows it.

Burying the pain of losing her friends and her professional swimming career in a terrorist attack, America's former sweetheart dulls her pain with drugs, pills and parties. The bomb left her with more than nightmares; shrapnel is lodged in her back and inching closer to her spinal cord. When the doctors tell her paralysis is inevitable, she decides to take her own life rather than face a lifetime in a wheelchair.

Mateo Butler isn't anyone's hero.

Reeling from the death of his little sister and his own cowardice, he spends his nights partying and his days ignoring the medical school acceptance letters and his parents' concerned phone calls. Just a couple of months from graduation, he's facing a future filled with shame and regret. The last thing he needs is to meet the woman who compels him to be a better man.

Can they save each other?

When Carlisle and Mateo meet, the chemistry between them is combustible. They play, party and hide their true selves until one night turns their lust into something more...something real. As secrets are revealed and walls collapse, what they were and what they might become doesn't matter as much as who they are together. When the choice comes down to life or death, can love be their salvation?

Buy it on the SALVATION page: http://robincovingtonromance.com/books/nashville-nights-series/salvation/.

ACKNOWLEDGMENTS

Huge, huge thanks to everyone who helped me get this book in your hands.

My best friends, Avery Flynn and Kimberly Kincaid, for keeping me on track and kicking my ass when necessary.

For the Sizzlemongers... I couldn't ask for a better group of friends. Not just a street team, we have become a group who support each other and I love that so hard.

The Main Man, Little Man and Lulu. My reasons to keep going, you are the fulfillment of a dream I didn't even know I had. I am a very lucky woman.

Dear Reader —

Thanks so much for reading my book. If you enjoyed this novella you can find out the latest info on my next release and enter for the monthly giveaway by signing up for my newsletter.

Newsletter sign up: http://bit.ly/1hde9GD

You can also drop me a line at robin@robincovingtonromance.com. I'd love to hear from you.

Xx,
Robin

Social Media Links:

Website: http://bit.ly/1lewhMg
Facebook Profile: http://on.fb.me/YSW9n3
Facebook Page: http://on.fb.me/1fCyWuQ
Twitter: @RobinCovington
Tumblr: http://robincovingtonromance.tumblr.com
Instagram: https://instagram.com/robincovington/
Pinterest: http://bit.ly/1c1Tm5u
Amazon Follow: http://amzn.to/1L2PrAG
Reader Group: http://on.fb.me/1hZdeEu

If you enjoyed REDEMPTION, check out my other
books:

A NIGHT OF SOUTHERN COMFORT
HIS SOUTHERN TEMPTATION
SWEET SOUTHERN BETRAYAL
PLAYING THE PART
SEX & THE SINGLE VAMP
PLAYING WITH THE DRUMMER
DARING THE PLAYER
TEMPTATION
SALVATION
THE PRINCE'S RUNAWAY LOVER
ONE LITTLE KISS
SECRET SANTA BABY
HER SECRET LOVER
RUSH